DAISY CHAIN WAR

Also in this trilogy:

Joan
O'Neill

DAISY CHAIN WAR

**Hodder
Children's
Books**

a division of Hodder Headline Limited

Text copyright © 1990 Joan O'Neill

First published in paperback in Ireland in 1990
by Attic Press

This paperback edition published in Great Britain in 2002
by Hodder Children's Books

The right of Joan O'Neill to be identified as the Author of
the Work has been asserted by her in accordance with
the Copyright, Designs and Patents Act 1988.

10 9 8 7 6 5 4 3 2 1

A Catalogue record for this book is available from
the British Library

ISBN 0 340 85466 9

Typeset by Avon Dataset Ltd, Bidford-on-Avon, Warks

Printed and bound in Great Britain by
Clays Ltd, St Ives plc

Hodder Children's Books
A Division of Hodder Headline Limited
338 Euston Road
London NW1 3BH

For my parents with love and gratitude

To a child dancing in the wind

Dance there upon the shore;
What need have you to care
For wind or water's roar?
And tumble out your hair
That the salt drops have wet;
Being young you have not known
The fool's triumph, nor yet
have lost as soon as won,
Nor the best labourer dead
And all the Sheaves to bind.
What need have you to dread
The monstrous crying of wind?

William Butler Yeats

Daisy Chains

They sat in the long grass braiding daisies, pinching each green stem carefully to make a hole without breaking it. They went faster, even working with their eyes closed sometimes.

Inch by inch they threaded the daisies and on and on, only stopping now and then to pick more bunches.

They made coronets for their hair, necklaces, bracelets and rings, until their fingers were yellow from the light dusty centres and tiny petals got caught under their fingernails as the long chains were woven.

They were so absorbed in their task that they didn't notice the sun sinking below the hills or the dusk settling in around them. They just kept pushing the stems, working them this way and that, their conversations sprinkled with their dreams of kings and queens and palaces and riches.

The evening air was heavy with the scent of summer's day end and the early stars twinkled shyly in the sky.

Then Gran's voice in the distance called out, 'Lizzie! Vicky! Come in at once.'

'Best go,' they said and unfolded themselves reluctantly.

'Make a wish,' Vicky commanded. 'You first.'

'I wish to grow up to be a beautiful princess and marry a prince.' Lizzie earnestly closed her eyes.

'What rubbish. Where will you ever meet a prince? I want to be a doctor and dissect bodies the way I'm dissecting these daisies. Now make another wish. A realistic one.'

'I wish Karen would come back and be safe here with us.' Lizzie bent her head so that Vicky wouldn't see the tears forming in her eyes.

'That's better.'

They crowned each other in solemn ceremony before making their way home, bedecked in their garlands of jewels. Sapphires and diamonds and rubies. Whatever form their imagination wanted the humble wilting daisies to take.

The star-studded sky cast a glow over them, picking out the contours of their childish features and the daisies in their hair.

'Vicky! Lizzie!' Gran called impatiently.

'Coming, Gran.'

'Your cocoa's growing a skin on it. What in the name of God are ye wearing?' Gran's eyes widened in amazement when she saw the pair of them.

'Precious jewels, Gran. And we've made a crown for you. Kneel down.'

Gran bent one stiff knee.

'This is as far as I'm going.'

'I crown you Queen of all the Grandmothers in Ireland.' Vicky placed the circle of daisies ceremoniously on her grandmother's head.

'You're daft.' Gran rose slowly and straightened herself up.

'But we love you.' Lizzie planted a kiss on her wrinkled cheek.

'Cut out the nonsense and go and wash yourselves before you sit down.' Gran sounded cross but her face was wreathed in smiles.

Lizzie

There'll be blue birds over
The white cliffs of Dover,
Tomorrow just you wait and see.
There'll be love and laughter,
And peace ever after,
Tomorrow . . .

G ran came to live with us at the beginning of
the war. I don't remember the exact day. But I
remember she was there when Karen was expected home
for her wedding. Not that her coming to live with us was
a cheerful time. Mam's efforts to make her welcome were
met with grumblings about her own place and having to
leave it.

Dad said, 'If war breaks out, here at least we know
you'll be safe with us.'

'I don't want to be a burden,' Gran replied, irritation
rising up in her.

'Ridiculous,' Mam said. 'You were ill and you never even
told us. I'd have brought you home sooner if I'd known.'

'That's what I was afraid of,' Gran rasped and then added, 'I didn't want anyone worrying about me,' an expression of pure martyrdom etched on her face. 'Anyway, I can take care of myself.'

Dad had told Mam that he'd discovered dirt everywhere in her cottage in County Limerick. Unwashed plates piled in the sink and saucepans encrusted with leftovers. Teeth steeping in a jar on the window-sill and Gran sitting in her old armchair with no fire in the hearth; just her coat fastened across her chest with a safety pin concealing the moth-eaten layers beneath.

'So unlike her. She took such pride in her home and her appearance,' he said.

It didn't take Gran long to settle in. Karen's arrival and the preparations for the wedding occupied our minds and we hardly noticed the odd half-mumbles from Gran as she talked to herself, a habit she had acquired from living alone for too long.

'We're going to Dublin tomorrow, Lizzie,' Mam said. 'So get to bed early.'

I held her hand tightly as we moved briskly through the crowded streets. Half walking, half running, trying to keep pace with her, we bustled and jostled our way.

This was our last trip to Dublin before the wedding and the 'arrangements' that Mam kept referring to were almost complete.

Now, laden with parcels, we made our way to Bewley's

to meet Karen. I sandwiched myself between them, listening to their excited chatter while spooning cream cake into my mouth.

There had been several weeks of hurried preparations ever since Karen wrote with the good news. Mam said it was a good job that she was getting married and I could tell that Karen too was very pleased. I was to be her flower girl and as Karen was my favourite person in the whole world, next to Mam and Gran of course, I was thrilled. Karen could only get home for a week before the wedding, so Mam and Gran had to do everything.

Gran baked the cakes. 'I never liked cooking for meself,' she said, rubbing in the butter with relish. 'Never got used to it.'

She iced the cakes with gnarled shaky hands. A delicate pink for the flowers on white satin icing. Proudly they were displayed in our front room where the family and guests would gather beforehand.

As our house filled with relations everyone was busy, except me.

'Go out to play until it's time for your fitting.' Mam was getting short-tempered with all the work that had to be done.

When the dressmaker arrived with her large circular hat-box full of accoutrements I shrank back from her. I dreaded the pinching and pulling, twisting me this way and that. She was like a conjuror. She talked to Mam endlessly, her mouth full of pins, all staying in position, like minute tin soldiers guarding huge white gates.

'Hold still,' she'd command and I obeyed, afraid to anger her in case she pricked me with one of her tin men.

'I'm doin' the weddin' for Rosie Moran. Big affair. Four bridesmaids and the train of the dress must be so many feet long. 'Course, her oul' fella's in the buildin' in England. Makin' a fortune. Nothin' spared for that one. She's marryin' a farmer. Plenty of land for the oul' lad to build on. Ha ha. Don't fret, I'll help 'em spend it. Very elaborate it'll be.'

Mam listened and nodded at intervals, not really interested in her tittle-tattle.

The night before the wedding Mam put me in a steaming bath and scrubbed me. Then Gran twisted my hair in rags and I was packed off to bed. I tossed and turned, unable to sleep, and wondered what Karen's young man was like. Would he be tall and handsome like his photograph? Would we like him? Would he make Karen happy? The drone of the voices downstairs faded and finally lulled me to sleep.

'Time you were up and dressed, Lizzie,' Mam called as the buttery sun streamed through my window. I threw back the blankets and watched the dust motes dance in the light before jumping out of bed.

'Come, child, eat your porridge,' Gran chided as I sat enthralled at all the activity in our kitchen.

After breakfast Mam combed my hair. She twisted huge sausage ringlets around her finger and gently slipped my new lace dress flecked with roses over my head. She carefully arranged the crown of rosebuds that matched my dress and laced up the new soft ballet shoes.

'Lovely,' she declared, giving me a squeeze. 'Wait downstairs with Dad.'

Dad stood in the hall. He looked taller in his new black suit. The white carnation in his buttonhole gave him a certain elegance.

'The cars are here,' he said, taking my hand.

Dad and Karen sat in front and I was squeezed between Mavis and Sadie, Karen's bridesmaids.

We drove to the church in the long sleek car and stood in the porch while Dad and Karen drove around in circles waiting for Paul to arrive.

'I hope he hasn't done a runner,' said Mavis.

'A what?' Sadie looked puzzled.

'You know, cleared off like.'

'Perish the thought,' Sadie shivered. 'I'm perished anyway.'

We laughed as we huddled together. Patrick, my cousin up from the country, was prancing about in hornpipe shoes, his velvet trousers only reaching below his knees. I didn't dare laugh. Mam would have killed me.

A few clouds raced across the clear blue sky and when Karen stepped out of the car on Dad's arm she looked just like one of the white fleecy clouds. We followed them slowly down the aisle as the organ played.

The sun, shining through the stained-glass windows, sent shafts of coloured light across the small procession, dazzling the diamonds in Karen's hair and the buttons on Paul's airforce uniform as he came to meet her from the front row of the church. He looked at her as if he had never seen her before, which was very strange, because they knew each other so well. He was more handsome than his photograph and held himself proud and straight. The candles on the altar danced and dipped merrily among the flowers like graceful ballerinas while Father Gilmartin, Dad's old school friend, said the mass. I held Karen's satin train and scattered petals from my little basket all the way from the altar, just as Mam had instructed me.

Joyful laughter rang out as the photographs were taken. Karen looked so happy that she glowed and showed off her new husband to everyone. Paul laughed, just as delighted with his new wife.

Then the photographs were taken and after that we drove to the big hotel on the seafront. Long tables were joined together in the ballroom and the wedding cake stood like a white and pink fairy castle in the centre of rows of orange juice in tall jugs. Relations and friends gathered and eyed one another from each end of the room. Waiters came and went with trays of filled glasses. Karen chatted happily to everyone but because I didn't know so many people I stayed with Patrick.

We sat down together for the breakfast and were astonished to find a dinner placed in front of us. Turkey, ham, and several vegetables.

'Funny breakfast,' Patrick said, dipping his fingers into his plate. I poked him in the ribs because Father Gilmartin had just stood up to talk. Several others spoke too, including Paul, who said that it was the happiest day of his life.

'I can't believe my luck. Karen's the most beautiful bride I ever set eyes on,' he said in the cowboy twang we knew from the cinema.

Everyone cheered and Karen blushed shyly when Paul hugged her.

After the meal the tables were cleared and pushed to one side. Paul and Karen led the dancing and looked so happy that it made my heart pound. Patrick raced me on to the floor and twirled me round and round until I was dizzy.

'You think you're a great dancer in those fancy shoes,' I said, 'but you look silly.'

He was furious and stormed off. Soon everyone was dancing except Patrick, who sulked in the corner. My Uncle Mike took me up for a reel and my cousin Eileen sang so sweetly that it made Gran shed a tear.

When it was time for Karen and Paul to leave they ran up the wide staircase to change. Karen turned, and threw her bouquet wide from her. It fell straight into my arms. I gasped with pleasure. Everyone cheered.

'Little Lizzie is next. Lizzie is next.'

We lined up to wave goodbye. A lump caught in my throat as I suddenly remembered that Karen was leaving again. Possibly for good this time. Then she was beside me hugging me tight and pressing a tiny box into my hand.

'Thanks, love. Thanks for being such a beautiful flower girl. I'll miss you. Now promise you won't be upset. We'll be home for the Christmas holidays.'

'I promise,' I said, squeezing her tight and glad she had someone as nice as Paul to look after her.

Then they were off, rattling down the drive of the hotel in their gaily painted car.

Mam wrapped me in her fur stole as the evening air grew chilly and I sat beside Gran on the way home.

''Twas a great day, Gertie,' Gran said to Mam as I busily opened the present Karen had given me.

A bracelet, gold and shiny, sat on a blue cushion. What a beauty, I thought as I slipped it on to my wrist, nudging Mam to look at it.

'I said wasn't it a great day, Gertie?' Gran raised her voice impatiently.

'It was, thank God.'

'And not a minute too soon,' Gran added. 'Did you notice Karen looked a bit plump in the dress?'

'Most wedding dresses have that effect,' sniffed Mam. 'I don't think anyone would have noticed.'

Dad gave her a dig with his elbow.

I listened as they talked on, but I knew why Karen looked plump. She was bursting with joy. Sure, didn't she tell me so herself.

Gran

Gran wasn't so thin and miserable any more. She made her brass bed every morning after breakfast and dusted the photograph of Grandad that she kept in a silver frame beside it.

'Poor soul,' Mam said. 'I must be tactful with her. It's just as well she came here before things got out of hand.'

Gran sang in a high cracked voice as she went about her chores and when she got tired she sat in her chair by the Aga. A chair roughened with age, with springs that creaked every time she moved. But she refused to sit anywhere else because her chair was the last remnant of her old home.

'Gertie,' she called, her eyes never leaving her furiously pecking knitting needles. 'That ham is cooked. I know by the smell of it.'

Mam moved to the range and lifted the lid of the black pot.

'Right as usual,' she said, testing the meat with a fork.

As the grandfather clock marked the hours in the corner I felt that time had slowed down for me. Karen had written to confirm she was coming home for Christmas and I couldn't wait.

'That's ninety pairs of socks,' Gran counted, turning another heel. 'And thirty pullovers.' Her face retained a mulish expression.

'If the troops don't go to war you'll be very disappointed,' Dad teased her.

'It's the least I can do. I'm lucky to have a roof over me head and a bit to eat and I'm in from the bitter cold. I know what it's like to live on bread and lard.' She looked him straight in the eye. 'Those poor soldiers are out there in the Curragh with no protection, all keyed up and ready for action. God help them.'

A shiver ran down my spine.

'Even if they don't get called to the front, sure they'll keep the enemy at bay.'

'What's two hundred and fifty thousand troops against Hitler's forces?' Dad said sarcastically.

'They're highly trained and skilled men and anyway de Valera won't let us go to war.'

'Ah, but you're forgetting Bill,' Mam chimed in. 'With this neutrality we're on our own now.'

She spoke with such sadness that I got afraid that something terrible was about to happen.

'Have sense, Gertie. Isn't it better to be on our own than have bombs raining down on our heads?' Gran's voice had a sharp edge to it.

'The support for neutrality is unanimous,' said Dad.

'Of course. 'Tis grateful we should be to Mr de Valera for his integrity.'

'You're a staunch de Valera woman, Ma,' Dad laughed.

'I wouldn't hear a word said against him. Have you finished your letter to Santa, Lizzie?'

'How do you spell cradle?' I asked, turning my attention to the grubby page in front of me.

'Never mind cradle. I doubt Santa will have such luxuries this year. Spell warm winter coat and you might have a better chance of getting it.'

'Talk of war and rumours of war makes people edgy.' Dad winked at me.

'C-r-a-d-l-e,' Mam spelt, slowly emphasising each letter, turning down the wireless.

20 December 1939

Dear Santa,
I would like a cradle for my doll Annie and a blanket and pillow. A rocking cradle so I can rock her to sleep. I would also like a bit of black draping to put over her at night to keep her safe from the bombs.
  Thank you and lots of love,
  Lizzie Doyle

'C'mon Lizzie and help me put up the rest of the decorations.'

I followed Dad upstairs to the freezing hall.

'Don't catch your death,' Gran called out after us. 'Have

you got your woolly vest on Lizzie? It's cold in this mausoleum of a place, Gertie. You have to keep movin' to keep warm.'

'Oh, Gran, don't exaggerate.' Mam's response was immediate but she made no fuss, dismissing Gran's caustic comments with a laugh.

From the hall I could hear them talking.

'She must miss Grandad,' I said to Dad.

'He's gone a long time now,' he shook his head. 'It didn't take much to make him happy. His pint of porter and his pipe after a day's work. Your Gran never made much of an effort to please him. She felt he was happy enough with the boys in the pub on a Friday night to bother about his "whims" as she called them. There was no pampering in those days. She worked too hard to think about other people's feelings. I don't ever remember them holding any conversation much. Always too busy. Of course, she's old now and crotchety and between you and me I think she's forgotten all about him.'

'Will she recognise him when she gets to heaven?'

Dad laughed. 'That's if he's there waiting for her. Though I'm sure he is. He was a good, hard-working man. The drop of drink was his only problem.'

We hung the coloured tinsel and put holly over the picture frames. The air was sweet with the smell of peat and the cooking ham.

Welcome Home Karen, in big red letters, was placed

over the vestibule door and each time I read it a thrill of excitement ran through me. Nothing could be more exciting for me. Not even the arrival of Santa Claus. As I watched the red corkscrew candles flickering on the Christmas tree I thought of Karen and the impending war, and realised how much I didn't really understand.

The house was so quiet after Karen left that I felt like an only child. Mam had lost a baby somewhere between Karen and me, leaving an age gap of ten years. I was a delicate child. My chest was so weak that Mam made me wear orange cotton wool stuff next to my skin, under my liberty bodice. When the doctor from the Health Board came to examine us in school the other girls laughed.

'Trying to pretend you're growin' diddies, Lizzie Doyle,' Biddy O'Rourke mocked.

I lurched for her to punch her on the nose but someone pulled me back.

'Take that scowl off your face, Lizzie, and sit down.' The teacher looked murderous.

Karen had grown up when Dad was working and things were more plentiful. He drove a car because he worked as a 'Compulsory Tillage Inspector'. We lived on Kingstown Terrace in one of a row of tall Georgian houses joined by a party wall. Some houses were drab, others had peeling paint. Some were falling down. But ours was always freshly painted cream with green window frames and doors. A flight of wide shallow steps led up to the hall door. The wrought-iron mud scraper was shiny silver. The upkeep of the house was important to Mam.

The carol singers knocked at the front door. I called down to Gran that they were waiting.

'Glory be. Get my purse.' She came quickly up the stairs.

'Give us a verse of "Away in a Manger",' she asked, while filling their box with rattling coins. Then she sang in full croaky voice along with them, putting them out of tune.

By now the snow blanketed the ground and Gran's eyes shone as she too caught my excitement.

'Come in before you get your death,' Mam called out.

Gran was in no hurry. She wouldn't leave until she got them to sing 'Silent Night'. Before she shut the door she showed me the evening star.

'It's beautiful, Gran.'

'It's celestial,' she said reverently. 'Now hurry up and make a wish.'

What more could I wish for in this magic world of my childhood, encircled by a love and warmth that reached out from within, strong enough to melt the icy snow and sustain me down all the years of my memory?

I looked at Gran standing there, her face smiling in a

million wrinkles, the hall light shining on her grey hair loosely caught up in a bun. The drab colours of her clothes were relieved by a bright flowery overall that gave her a kind of gaiety. I watched her talk to the carol singers, her excitement infectious as she shuffled around them all in carpet slippers a size too big, because her feet swelled up sometimes.

'You're wonderful to come out and sing in the cold,' she said. 'But sure it's such a wonderful feast. The birth of Christ himself.' Her eyes gazed up to heaven, suddenly young and bright and full of enquiry.

I wished for Karen's safe homecoming just as Mam came up into the hall.

'Gran, come in,' she said gently. 'And it's bed for you, my little lady.'

'You'd better get plenty of sleep if you're to enjoy yourself tomorrow,' Gran said. 'We're going to Dublin to do the Christmas shopping.'

Gran was first on the tram, clutching the rail grimly.

'Watch your step, Lizzie,' she called over her shoulder. 'These bloody trams are lethal. They go so fast,' she told the conductor, fumbling in her bag for the fare. 'Nelson's Pillar. Two adults and a child.'

'Shopping?' he asked her.

Gran nodded, holding on to the rail for dear life.

'Fourpence each and half for the child.' He rolled out the tickets from his machine. Then he caught her by the arm and guided her to a seat by the window. Mam squeezed me in beside her and sat in front just as the tram began to whine into action.

We began our shopping in Pims' in George's Street where the basement was a wonderland of toys. Santa roamed around talking to the children.

'Post your letter early and send it to the North Pole.'

'Will you still be able to come to Ireland, even though there's war?' I asked him, because we had been told in school that the British Army was on full alert and he had to cross England to get here.

He laughed a jolly ho ho and assured me he'd arrive on Christmas eve, war or no war.

'Pick out what you want, now,' he said and I went off to examine the fancy dolls and prams and cowboy outfits with guns and holsters.

A huge Santa waving from his sleigh hung over McBirney's, down the Quays, where we went to get Gran's special crochet hooks and cottons.

'We'll have a spot of dinner here, Gertie. The child must be starving,' Gran said.

She marched us into the restaurant.

'This is my treat.' She took out her glasses to look at the menu.

We ordered chicken and ham and apple tart to follow.

'Give the child a glass of lemonade please, and two teas,' she commanded the young waitress.

'You're not paying this bill,' Mam argued, but Gran insisted, counting out five whole shillings, the exact amount.

They checked their lists before we left McBirney's and made our way to Woolworth's for the stocking fillers and more candles for the Christmas tree. Mam bought a turkey in Moore Street. The city was bare and cold as we headed for Nelson's Pillar to get the tram. It was getting dark and Santa in his sleigh over McBirney's was lit up now in red, yellow and white fairy lights. As the queue for the number eight lengthened, Gran had a sudden urge to go to the toilet.

'I'll be back in a minute.' She went off round the corner. I shivered with the cold.

'Where could she have got to?' said Mam after a few minutes, looking around anxiously.

After a while the buses and trams for the different routes arrived. The queues lengthened. There was still no sign of Gran.

'Sure, the toilet is only over there.' Mam was agitated. 'Wait here, don't move. I'm going over to get her.'

She returned a few minutes later, shaking her head.

'She's not there. Could she have got on the wrong tram?' She was watching the trams that were pulling out.

Fear gripped me as Mam questioned one conductor after another and then went to the inspector's office. He sent for the garda who was marching up and down the street and sudden panic rose up among the crowd. Gran was missing. What a wretched end to a lovely day. I was tired. My feet hurt and I wanted to cry, but I was sorry for Mam because a dark flush came over her face and I knew something awful was happening.

'Oh, that stupid woman,' she cried as everyone milled around and the queues became disordered as the search for Gran got under way.

'Of course, she's old,' she said, making excuses out of sheer embarrassment to the inspector.

'When people get old, there's no accounting for what they might do.' He nodded his head wisely as he wrote in a book, but Mam found no comfort in that remark.

Eventually we went home by ourselves on the advice from garda headquarters who had by now sent a search party all over the city to try and find Gran. The journey home was slow and lonely. Supposing Gran had been killed by a tram or a big dray horse? I began to cry.

'Hush,' Mam said. 'They'll find your gran and when I get her home I'll give her a piece of my mind.'

'Suppose she's d-e-a-d.' I spelled it out, my lips trembling as I squeezed my eyes shut, hardly bearing to think about it.

'Don't let your imagination run away with you. She probably just lost her way. They'll find her and next time I'll tie a rope around her if we're going anywhere. What am I going to tell your father? He'll never believe me that I lost her.'

There were two red blotches on Mam's cheeks; the rest of her face was chalk white.

'She lost herself, Mam.'

'That's a great comfort.'

When we got home, we found Gran asleep in her chair, snoring loudly, her cheeks flushed.

'Gran,' Mam shouted, shaking her, but she couldn't rouse her. 'Gran, wake up. You gave us a terrible fright. Where did you get to?'

Finally Gran came to and looked around uncertainly.

'Is that the time already?' she said slurring her words, and when she went to get up out of her chair her movements were awkward.

'Did you have an accident, Gran?' I asked.

'How did you get home? We were worried stiff.'

'I'm stiff meself,' she said dragging her legs as she went for the kettle. 'It's only rheumatism. But, sure, who'd be bothered with an old woman and her complaints.'

'Gran,' Mam shouted. 'We were worried sick.'

Gran looked back sheepishly, her red-veined face heightened to the colour of her cheeks.

'I went for a little drop to warm meself. Sure, there's no harm in that. Only when I got back you weren't there. I thought I'd better get the next tram home.'

Mam opened and closed her mouth, hardly trusting herself to speak.

'Wait till Bill hears about this,' she said. 'Lizzie, get

ready for bed. I'll bring your supper up to you. You're exhausted.'

Dad came in just as I left the kitchen. I stood listening at the door.

'Bill, your mother drinks. Did you know that?'

I heard Mam's raised voice and Gran's protestations. It was my first warning about the 'little weakness' Gran had. A weakness that was never mentioned outside our home and rarely within its walls.

Next morning Gran was sitting in her room facing the window, the shutters half open. She looked ill.

'Are you all right, Gran?' I asked, my eyes on her shaking hands.

''Course I'm all right. Come in,' she said, her indignation fading. 'Such a lot of nonsense. I only had a drop. As if that made any difference. I used to make wine meself, you know. Elderberry. It isn't a crime to take a little drop.' Her tone was defensive, but there was an agitated despair in her voice and tears in her eyes. 'I got a rare mouthful from your dad. They'll never let me out again after this.' A frown creased her brow.

'You'll still go to mass won't you and shopping with me?' I was afraid I'd start to cry too and disgrace myself.

She brightened up. 'Of course I will,' she said more robustly. 'We've still things to get for Christmas, and wild horses wouldn't keep me out of the church. Let's see. Where's that list?' She rooted in her bag for her glasses, tapping her yellow teeth with her pencil. She was her old self again.

At half past nine she came downstairs in her ordinary hat and coat.

'I'm off to mass, Gertie,' she called as if nothing had happened. 'Are you coming Lizzie? I have to keep moving, this house is bitter cold. Now what do you want, Gertie? Bread? Butter? Tea? Sugar?'

'You won't be able to carry all that home.'

'Lizzie will help me, won't you?' she winked at me just as Mam turned and caught her eye.

'I want to be straight with you, Gran.' Mam's voice was gentle. 'I don't mind you going downtown. And I don't want you to feel you have to do jobs here either. You can take things easy. Sit on your backside all day if you like. Only come home after you've done the shopping.'

She spoke kindly, cleansed of enmity towards the old woman who stood looking vague, innocently adjusting the greeny-brown plumes on her felt hat.

'Must be off,' was all Gran said. 'Get your coat, Lizzie.'

Gran's expectations weren't really high and she was willing to give everything in return.

'I have my ration books and my pension. We'll get the necessities,' she said as we went into Pay and Take.

'I never starved in my life and nobody belonging to me either. Though I've lived on the edge of it by times.' Mr King, the manager, ticked off her pink ration books and wrapped the messages in brown tissue paper.

'Terrible shortages,' he complained. 'Can't get oranges or bananas. Everything's scarce.'

'As long as we have the tea, to hell with the oranges.' Gran didn't mince her words. 'Aren't we fortunate to have our health and strength and be safe from that oul' Hitler fella who's raging war on everyone. Only for Mr de Valera he'd be here too. Grand man, Mr de Valera. Grand man. Oh, and by the way Mr King, if you do get any extra tea in, keep a grain aside for me.' She knew Mr King was a member of the Fianna Fáil party.

'I will, to be sure, Mrs Doyle, and here's a little something for yourself and the family for Christmas.'

He handed her a bottle of wine and my heart sank.

'For your mother, Lizzie, with the compliments of the season,' he said, wrapping a tin of biscuits in red crêpe paper.

'Thank you.'

I took the biscuits and Gran said, 'You're a gentleman Mr King. A real gent.'

When we got home Gran handed over the bottle of wine and Mam put it away in the cupboard for Christmas.

Christmas eve was bitterly cold.

'Can't I wait up for Karen?' I pleaded.

'It could be all hours before she arrives. You'd be jaded tomorrow.'

I didn't want that, so I let Mam tuck me in with the stone warming jar at my feet.

'Have you hung up your stocking?' Then she laughed when she saw one of Gran's army socks at the foot of the bed.

'Call me early, don't forget.'

She pulled down the black sateen over the blind, shutting out the bright stars and plunging me into darkness.

'Of course I won't,' she said, bending to kiss me goodnight.

As she left the room I could hear Dad downstairs getting ready to go to meet the mailboat.

Christmas morning dawned bright and very cold. I stood in the hall, tears streaming down my face, putting on my new coat, my fingers awkwardly trying to fit the buttons into the tight buttonholes. Gran stooped to tie my shoelaces properly.

'Now don't take on so, Lizzie,' she said. 'It's not the end of the world.'

I concentrated on the shiny colours of the new pheasant feather in her hat, trying to stop crying.

'Karen must have missed the boat. The routes are all upside down,' Dad said. 'Or maybe it was overcrowded. There are fewer sailings now.'

No words could comfort me. I hated the mention of the war. To me it spelt shortages and discomfort and worried looks passing between Mam and Dad. All during mass I thought of Karen and prayed her boat hadn't been bombed.

A week later Karen's letter arrived telling us her leave had been cancelled. The hospital was on full alert because of the war. It was the longest week of my life.

John

I was lonely for Karen. It seemed ages since her wedding.

'Cheer up,' Mam said. 'Karen won't be away for too long. She's coming home to have the baby.'

'Baby? What baby?'

'Karen's having a baby soon and you know what that means?' Mam asked.

'It means we'll be a disgrace in the parish if she comes home too soon,' Gran mumbled under her breath.

'It means,' Mam continued, pretending not to hear her, 'that you'll be an auntie.'

'Me! An auntie!' I couldn't believe my ears.

'We won't be able to raise our heads,' Gran muttered to herself.

'Now, Gran.' Mam was defensive. 'Karen's always welcome home. Welcome in her own home,' she repeated for emphasis. 'No matter what the circumstances. Anyway, Bill wants her home. London is too dangerous and Paul is away most of the time.'

'Part of the trouble with you, Gertie, is that you spoilt

her. You thought she could do no wrong.'

'Yes – well. C'mon Lizzie. Out to play with you. This conversation is not for your ears.'

'We never had any trouble like that on our side,' Gran sniffed, stabbing her crochet hook furiously in and out of the fine white shawl she was making.

'That's enough, Gran.' Mam was cross now. I couldn't understand why Gran was annoyed with Karen. It was great news. I couldn't wait.

'Karen is going to have a baby,' I said to my pal May Tully.

May Tully was tying a long rope in a double knot to our railings. She was tall for her age and lanky, her long dark hair plaited in two neat plaits and tied with white matching bows.

'I know.' She secured the knot and looked past me, a knowing look in her measuring eyes.

'Who told you?' She always seemed to know everything but this news had surprised even me.

'Nobody,' she said importantly. 'I heard my mother and Mrs Scanlon talkin'. Everybody is talkin'.'

'It's very exciting. And guess what?'

'What?' she said indulgently, humouring me.

'I'm going to be an auntie.'

She grinned, showing her crooked teeth, then walked the distance of the rope, holding it firmly in her hand.

'Are we playin' skippin' or not?' she said impatiently.

I kicked a stone and looked away, not really wanting to play with her.

She guessed.

'Anyway. My mother says your Karen is a disgrace.'

I stared at the full-blown roses and fading lupins in our garden, then closed my eyes to wait for the black receding patch of temper to focus back into colour again. It didn't and when I opened my eyes and saw that crooked mocking smile and her rabbity buck teeth, I moved forward and slapped her stupid lumpy face. Then I pulled one of her neat plaits.

She scowled and her eyes bulged as a look of disbelief overtook her features. How had I dared hit the leader of our gang?

Without question she was the authority on every known subject in our terrace, just because she was two years older than the rest of us and had two older brothers who'd emigrated to England.

'You'll pay for this, Lizzie Doyle. Wait and see.'

Then she ran home bawling to her mother.

Mam came running out of the house.

'Lizzie, you shouldn't have done that. What possessed you?'

'She called Karen a disgrace.' I stood my ground, stubborn and staring.

Mrs Tully came up the road, her jaws sucked in, her eyes blazing. She had her hands clenched into fists by her sides. May straggled behind snivelling.

'Say you're sorry quick, or there'll be hell to pay,' Mrs Tully hissed, a few dark hairs on her chin wiggling as she spoke.

'Sorry,' I muttered, but I wasn't.

May grinned spitefully at me, then laughed a high giddy laugh.

'Look, she's trying not to cry.' She pointed her finger at me. 'She's frightened though. Cowardy cowardy custard, stick your head in mustard!'

'Go boil your . . .'

'C'mon home.' Her mother dragged her by the arm. 'You're not playin' with the likes of that one. Young bastards is all they're fit for rearin'.'

Black spots danced before my eyes but Mam grabbed me and pushed me inside when I tried to lunge at May again. I wanted to pull her silly plaits off her head and make a skipping rope out of them, with her dangling on the end. 'Upstairs with you,' Mam shouted. 'Peel off all your clothes till I give you a good scrubbing. And I'll wash your mouth out with salt if you ever behave like that again.'

'What's up?' asked Gran anxiously.

'She hit May Tully and pulled her hair.'

'Never!' Gran's eyes widened.

'She did.'

'She said horrible things about Karen.' I lifted my chin.

'Didn't I tell you, Gertie, this would bring nothing but trouble.'

32

I ran upstairs, Mam following me.

'She's rude. I hate her.'

I looked in terror at the wooden spoon in her hand.

'Peel off your clothes and get into that bath.'

She caught me on the bare backside with the edge of the spoon and I roared.

'Keep away from that crowd. They've no class.' She raised the spoon again then dropped it, tears in her eyes. Filling the bath with steaming water she lathered the facecloth with Pear's soap until its dull brown colour was transformed into a clear burnished gold. She scrubbed me, her aggression leaving red weals on my pale skin.

'Next time I'll skelp the living daylights out of you.' She was red-faced and perspiring.

'Sorry.' I was glad of the lucky escape.

'You'll have to control that temper of yours, Lizzie,' Gran said, her blue eyes puzzled behind her reading glasses.

A lump rose in my throat which I swallowed and glared at her.

'It's not my fault. She's horrible. It's not fair.'

Gran spoke reasonably. 'If you can't get on with her, keep away. Now go upstairs and bring down my white crochet cotton. I'll show you how to do the chain stitch.'

As I left the kitchen I heard her say to Mam, 'Don't be too hard on her, Gertie, she's not entirely to blame. It's only natural things will be said in the circumstances. It'll all settle down and Lizzie's a good child underneath.'

I didn't go out to play for a while but I was angry for ages. It was a different anger than the one I felt when someone tried to make me do things I didn't like doing. May Tully made me angry just by existing, with the bossy way she talked and the way she made the others play the games she wanted to play.

One morning Mam said to me, 'Karen's home. Came late last night.'

I bounded up the stairs and into her room calling 'Karen, Karen' at the top of my voice.

'Hello, love,' she said, putting out her hands to me. 'Oh be careful. I'm not able for all this energy.'

She laughed, holding me off as I went to throw myself on her bed.

'You're going to have a baby!'

'Yes,' she smiled. 'You'll help me look after it, won't you?'

'Of course I will, you don't have to ask.'

She looked pale and she didn't tumble me in the air like she usually did.

We went for walks, Karen and me, always in the evenings just before dark. She wasn't as tall as I'd remembered. She seemed lower, nearer the ground, and she walked slowly and heavily. I knew by the way she looked into the middle distance that it was something to do with Paul and the baby that she was thinking about. She didn't talk much or laugh any more. I was about to ask her where Paul was when she said, 'I'm sorry I couldn't get home for Christmas, Lizzie. I was disappointed too but we had to pitch in. Even the nurses who'd already gone on leave were recalled.'

'You're here now. That's all that matters.' I smiled up at her and noticed her brush a tear from her cheek.

'She's sad and not very well,' I said to Mam.

'She's far too thin. That's what she is.' Gran always had the last word.

It was silly to say Karen was thin. She was huge, so swollen that she waddled like a duck.

As time went by Karen grew even more quiet. I wouldn't tell Pauline Byrne or Tess Mathews or Annie Duggan why May and me weren't speaking. At the corner shop we all bought liquorice allsorts, honey bees and peg's legs, then they walked home with May. I lagged behind, chewing all the way up the back lane.

It was the last day of school and we were celebrating. Our back lane divided the coach houses and Meany's farm. It was a narrow path, dry and dusty from the heat. Bordered by larch poplars and overhanging birch trees, it was cool on hot days. Weeds grew along the dividing wire. Mam picked the abundance of nettles for soup, wearing Dad's old driving gloves to protect her hands. The lane was quiet. Only the boys playing truant from school would gather around the old iron gate for a sneaky fag after robbing Mrs Green's orchard. The lane was a forbidden place to most of us children but as we walked along, clumped together sharing out our booty, the whole summer stretched before us. Time was endless and it was ours. On the first day of the holidays no one would say a word to us.

But it was in the evening that I liked the laneway best of all. When the sun was setting, casting long shadows across the fields, and the cows, heavy with milk, waited patiently. I would sit in the little wicker chair in the loft over our coach house and wait for Dad's return. When I spied him far down the lane I would race down the rickety stairs, lift the latch on the gate and run to meet him. He would hoist me up on to his shoulders where I caught a glimpse of the distant golf course, and imagined a wonderful world beyond, as he carried me home.

I stayed in a lot to help, which was a good excuse not to encounter May Tully. I brought Karen up her breakfast and did jobs for her. I sat in the sunshine watching Mam wring out the sheets through the old mangle, her strong arms pulling them wide from her, little jets of water spouting from them. We hung them on the line. We loved to watch them billowing in the strong breeze.

Then we'd fold them, stretching and pulling, me holding tightly against Mam's strength. We dragged out carpets and mats to the clothesline, beating them furiously with the carpet beater.

And all the time I was thinking of Karen's baby. Trying to imagine what he or she would be like.

'We can't bring a brand new baby into a house that isn't spotless, and you're a great little helper,' Gran would say.

I loved the praise and couldn't do enough for her so I could hear it again.

'When is Karen going to have the baby, Gran?'

'Don't bother me with questions and don't vex your mother either.'

'She doesn't mean any harm.' Mam came into the kitchen while we were setting the table for tea.

I never wanted to go to bed these days. All I wanted was to be with Karen. I often sat watching her brushing her long hair, her face half covered and mysterious. She was thinking her own secrets.

'I wish it was all over,' she sighed one evening.

She was distant as if she didn't belong to us any more. I mentioned this to Mam. She thought for a minute.

'She has a lot on her mind.'

Then I began to cry.

'Hush now. There's nothing to cry about. Karen's in no real trouble. And if you're a good girl I'll take you shopping with me tomorrow.'

'Wake up,' Mam whispered. I crept downstairs, my clothes under my arm. 'We won't disturb the others. Eat up and we'll be off.'

We walked to the station and took the train to the city. We dodged the crowds, the smells of the dray horses and the clip clop of hooves as we made our way to Clery's.

Mam bought several skeins of fine white wool to knit vests and matinee coats for the baby and a length of material for a loose frock for Karen. A red-faced, jolly woman served us and wished Mam luck when she told her she was going to be a grandmother.

'Look at that dress, Mam.'

It was white with puffed sleeves and embroidered edges, waisted with a blue satin ribbon that tied in a bow at the back.

'It'd be grand for the christening all right,' she said, counting out her pound notes.

We went through back alleyways to Moore Street. Mam bought apples and pears and bananas from Rosie on the corner.

'Tuppence each the oranges, eight for a shillin'. The blessin's of God be on ye and yers, Missus.'

She gave me an orange to 'suck on the way home'.

'Were ye up at the Park?' she asked Mam. 'It's lined with turf. Never saw the likes of it in all me life. They must be expectin' a helluva winter.' She blew her nose in her sleeve, almost pre-empting the cold.

'They're gettin' ready for the war, that's what they're doin',' the woman on the next stall said. 'Mark my words, it's not for nuttin' they're making walls outa turf.'

'Bless de Valera,

Bless MacEntee,

Give us the brown bread,

38

And half packet of tea,' Rosie sang.

'But no whiskey, I'll grant you,' someone chimed in and they all laughed in cheerful misery.

I told Karen about our day, noticing that she looked much better.

'Listen, don't tell anyone. But I've had some news. Paul wrote and he's found us a lovely little house. After the baby is born and the wretched war is over he's sending for us. He thinks the war will be over soon. The word is that 1941 should see the end of it.'

Suddenly I felt cold and sad. That night I lay in bed listening to their voices downstairs, to the falling rain and the wild wind blowing outside, and I didn't want to let her go back. Karen got a sudden pain in her back early one morning. Then it started in her tummy. Mam got the suitcase out of the wardrobe and Dad went for a taxi. I began to feel alarmed. Gran stood solemnly in the hall, her rosary beads passing swiftly through her fingers.

'If you'd say a prayer for your sister instead of hopping around like a flea you might do her some good.'

Karen came down in her slippers, wrapped in her coat, her nightdress dipping below the hem. Mam was fussing behind her with the case. Dad took her arm, giving her hand a squeeze and I remembered her wedding and wished Paul were with us. I remembered how they'd laughed together and danced. How happy they had been. Now her face looked flushed and empty.

'Goodbye, Karen.' I ran to her.

She held me tight to her.

'I won't be away too long. When I come home everything will be back to normal.' She lifted my chin with her finger.

Gran threw her eyes up to heaven.

'Take care of your gran, love. We won't be back for a while,' Mam called before the door shut behind her.

'How do people get babies?' I asked Gran as she set the table.

'Never you mind, missie. You'll know soon enough.'

'Ah Gran,' I coaxed.

'Keep your tongue in your head and mind your manners. You're far too young to think about these things.' She sounded annoyed but there was a softness in her expression.

Dad came home alone and sat silently in the corner reading his newspaper as if he was afraid one of us might ask him a question and disturb the peace. I went out to play because Gran made me but I hung around our gate afraid to go far in case I met May Tully or missed Mam coming home.

'Come to the shop with me,' Jimmy Scanlon said, but I wouldn't.

'I have to sweep the steps,' I pretended and made a grand gesture of getting the brush, starting at the hall door and working down each step, carefully brushing all the dirt into a neat pile. I had reached the path before Mam came up the street, smiling broadly.

'How's Karen, Mam?'

'Fine.' She leaned against the gate, shutting it with her back.

'Did she . . .'

'She did indeed. A beautiful baby boy.' She shifted her bags of shopping from one hand to the other in a tired gesture.

I wanted to tell all my pals but I decided not to. I wouldn't satisfy May Tully with the news.

Dad took Gran and me to see Karen and the baby.

'Only a little peep, mind,' Mam warned. 'Karen will be tired.'

Gran brought the white shawl and I brought the chocolates.

Gran hugged Karen. 'Now tell me all about it. Were the pains bad?' She sat beside her. 'Bill, take Lizzie to see the new baby.'

I didn't even get a chance to say hello to Karen.

He was the tiniest baby I'd ever seen. A scrap with a button nose and fingers like a star-fish. Suddenly he opened his eyes. They were deep blue, the colour of the sea.

'Oh Dad. Look. He's lovely, isn't he?'

Dad held him a moment before the nurse took him back, and declared him perfect.

Gran joined us and shook holy water from her Lourdes bottle all around him.

'That'll keep the devil away from him until he's baptised. And by the way, when is the christening?'

'Just as soon as Paul gets home.' Dad answered quietly so as not to disturb the baby.

But Paul wasn't at the christening. Three days beforehand a letter arrived telling Karen that he was on secret missions and couldn't get leave of absence. He would write again soon.

'Why is Paul's work a secret?' I asked Gran.

'It's the Emergency, or "the war" as they know it. He's an airforce pilot. But the war will be over soon. So they say. Then everything will be back to normal.'

Paul wrote a longer letter explaining that air raids were expected on London and major cities in England. Children had already been evacuated to the south of England. Germany had invaded the lowlands, he said, and the airforce was the first line of defence.

'Our performance will settle it all,' he wrote.

I knew all about the Emergency. I knew about the shortages and the pink ration books. The condensed milk we had to use curdled the tea and tasted sweet and horrible and the grey bread gave our insides a good 'turnout' as Gran said.

'Paul will be here soon enough to see his lovely little son.' Gran sounded convincing. 'Now see if Karen wants the feed for the baby and don't pester her with questions.'

'Even if Paul can't come, we'll have the christening just the same,' said Mam.

'Poor Karen will miss it too. She hasn't been churched yet,' Gran reminded us.

'Such a lot of nonsense.' Mam looked cross. 'Poor Karen considered "unclean" just because she gave birth. It's an old pagan custom.'

Gran sighed in acceptance.

'Churching is a load of rubbish.' Mam stormed off out to the clothesline.

All the family and relations gathered again in the little church. It was just like the wedding only without the bride and groom. Father Gilmartin congratulated them in their 'temporary absence' and welcomed us all. The ceremony was short. Sadie, Karen's bridesmaid, held the baby, who was lost in a long silk robe, flounced and ruched with lace around his tiny neck and wrists.

'Thank God he's peaceful,' Gran sighed, the pheasant feather on her new felt hat nodding up and down in approval.

Father Gilmartin said the prayers and poured a jug of water over the baby's head.

'I baptise you, John William Paul.'

The baby's face turned red then blue and he howled his torment, his tiny face screwed up, his mouth a wide O.

'Hush there.' Sadie held and rocked him, trying to soothe him.

'Too much water,' Mam whispered.

'He'll need all he can get.' Gran raised her eyes to heaven.

Afterwards we all went back to the house. Patrick was

there, his trousers too long this time. Mary Doyle, my cousin, had long pigtails. Her blue eyes danced and she thought she was beautiful. Everybody brought presents. Despite the Emergency, there was chicken and ham, and trifle in a huge fancy bowl. Tinned fruit and jelly and cream. Dozens of sandwiches and one of the iced cakes from Karen's wedding. The men drank bottles of stout and chanted 'long legs to the baby' as they raised their glasses.

'That baby will be the tallest man in Ireland.' Gran was eyeing the empty bottles stashed in the corner.

I wore my beautiful new dress and the lace stockings Gran had made for me, and the black patent shoes with straps across them. Karen sat quietly holding her baby, her face a mixture of sadness and pride.

In the evening when everyone was gone home I sat curled up on Dad's knee in the big armchair. The fire was blazing though it was a mild evening.

There was a knock on the door.

'It's the post,' Mam said.

'What! At this hour?' Dad went to the door.

He returned with a telegram for Karen.

Pale, with shaking fingers she tore it open.

Paul was missing in action, presumed dead, it said.

There was no consoling her. I wanted to say the right words to comfort her, but I knew that there weren't any I could think of. She stayed in bed. She wouldn't eat the tasty morsels Mam sent me up with. Her eyes were swollen pools of sadness. The whole neighbourhood came to sympathise, except, of course, the Tullys.

'She won't be leaving us now,' I whispered to Gran.

'Shhh,' she said. 'I knew no good would come of her going to England to do nursing. But they wouldn't listen to me. Meeting up with strangers.'

'Paul wasn't a stranger, Gran,' I protested. 'He was friendly.'

'A bit too friendly if you ask me,' she muttered under her breath, but I heard her.

Our house was a silent, unhappy house.

'Anyway, we have baby John.'

'That's true and a fine little fellow he is. God help him without a father in this big wide world.'

Death didn't mean as much to me as it did to all of them. As far as I was concerned I had Karen home for good and that was all that mattered.

Karen didn't improve with time. She became frantic.

She wrote to the War Office in London saying that somebody must know where to find him. She was distraught.

'I have no idea where to look for him myself,' she said. She didn't even know where he was posted. 'Damn this stupid war and damn their secret missions.'

She begged the War Office for more information about Paul's whereabouts. Gran said she plagued them. All she received in return was a polite letter assuring her that they would contact her as soon as they had any further information. She never heard from them again. 'Missing in action' was their final word.

She refused to believe that Paul could just disappear. But it was the lack of information that tormented her. She felt she should be doing more to find him but didn't know where to begin.

'It's a pretty stiff letter,' said Dad.

'They're a pretty stiff crowd.' Gran spoke through clenched teeth. But then Britain wasn't her favourite country.

'Karen's in a deep depression. What can we do to help her?' Mam was very worried.

It seemed no one knew anything about Paul and if they did they were deliberately not telling her. She alternated between deep depression, convinced that he was dead, and a ray of hope that surfaced on a good day, if John William smiled at her perhaps.

Her faint hope wavered and disappeared. As time went on her anguish and hopelessness made us all very anxious. Gran cursed the war and the system that delivered terse news bulletins like the one Karen got. But she kept praying. She urged Karen to pray but she couldn't convince her.

'I can't go on without him. I can't. Why was he taken and I was left alone?'

'You're not alone.'

I felt the emptiness inside her head. I felt the sick feeling she was feeling. I was afraid for her.

'I'm being tortured. Grindingly and slowly tortured. And I don't understand why.'

Vicky

Our home was in chaos when another crisis put Karen's grief temporarily into the background.

Auntie Sissy, Gran's only daughter, wrote from London that she was 'entrusting' her ten-year-old daughter, Victoria, into Gran's safekeeping for the duration of the war.

At the beginning of July the Battle of Britain was fought out in the skies over the south-east corner of England. Belgium and France had fallen and British and German fighter planes battled it out each day.

Auntie Sissy said that only the British cabinet and Fighter Command knew how close they came to being defeated.

The news was censored but we heard snippets of Mr Churchill's encouraging speeches doled out to the unfortunate citizens, at suitable intervals, throughout the duration of the war. 'Never in the history of human conflict has so much been owed by so many to so few.'

'Sissy always suffered from delusions of grandeur,' said Gran. 'I warned her not to marry Hermy. Marry an Irish man, I told her. Stick to your own kind. But there was no talking sense into her. Now look at the predicament she's in. Poor little Victoria not safe because she's Jewish.'

'No, they're evacuating all the children,' Dad explained. 'This war is really getting dirty now. Bombings all night long. It's nothing to do with the fact that she's Jewish. But it'll give the children a holiday and a chance to see the countryside. Couldn't be pleasant in London.'

'Holiday indeed! Kind of Hitler to arrange this war to give the poor children a holiday.'

That's how we came to be standing at Dun Laoghaire harbour waiting for the arrival of the mailboat on a hot sticky day in August.

I had saved my pocket money for little treats for her and, as the boat slowly came into view, excitement gripped me. Victoria was less than a year older than me. I had been planning days of great adventure for us from the moment I heard she was coming. Picnics at the seaside. Treasure hunts in the back lane. (Surely Mam would make an exception for Victoria?) Cowboys and Indians with the gang. But when I saw her standing there, an ugly black rubber gas-mask hitting off her knobbly knees, her cardboard suitcase secured with string tightly clutched to her, a big label around her neck with her name written on it, my heart sank. An overwhelming sense of betrayal was my strongest emotion as I watched this skinny waif with huge eyes hollowed out of a skeletal face. How

49

could I introduce this miserable girl with lanky hair and dressed in a raggy school uniform to the gang as my cousin Victoria from London? Wouldn't May Tully have a right laugh?

Then as Dad bent to kiss her cheek she burst into tears, howling that she didn't want to come to live with strangers and that she wanted to go home.

I was furious at her ingratitude. Weren't we saving her life by taking her in, giving her shelter? Hadn't we enough problems without her crying all over the place? Then guilt overtook me as she stared at me in hostile wonderment. She must feel very strange, I thought, and went to help carry her case.

'Hello, Victoria,' I said, reading her name off the label. VICTORIA ROSENBLUME. 'I'm Lizzie.'

'Vicky,' she sniffed. 'My name's Vicky.'

Her voice was barely audible. What would Gran make of her, I wondered, as we drove home in the taxi.

'What a little darlin' you are,' Gran greeted her. 'Imagine Sissy's own little girl come to visit her old gran,' she said, hugging her and pushing her away from her, saying, 'Let me have a good look at you.'

A stab of jealousy pierced me. What if Gran were to get really fond of her? But that was impossible. She was nothing like what Gran had imagined Auntie Sissy's daughter to be. If Sissy had delusions of grandeur they weren't evident in her offspring. This pale child with a nose you could wallpaper and tracks of sea-sick around her mouth wasn't in the least endearing. Gran was just being kind.

Mam took her upstairs to the bedroom that she was going to share with me for the duration of her stay, while Gran prepared the tea. She had baked scones and fruit cake and was making fairy sandwiches. It was like a party.

'She doesn't take after Sissy, that's for sure. I could see Hermy the minute I laid eyes on her. Poor little thing. Wrapped up like a parcel.'

'At least she had an address to be sent to. Most of them haven't,' Dad said, his eyes never leaving the newspaper he was reading.

When Vicky came downstairs her hair was wet and lank around her head. She was wearing my dressing-gown and slippers.

'Sit here beside me, lovey, and tell me all about yourself,' Gran told her. She seemed more comfortable with Gran and told her about the 'Blitz'.

'Sounds shocking. I'm glad you're safe with us. Your mother should have come too.'

'She's working in a munitions factory. Says she must do her bit to help out.' Vicky's lip trembled.

'Hm. Always had strange notions.'

Dad threw her a look of disapproval. 'And your dad? Is he staying on in London too?'

'Oh no. He's gone to Canada as a war guest. He hopes to find work and send money to help Mum out.'

'I see.' This time Gran remained tight-lipped. But I

heard her say to Dad later, 'Typical Hermy. Always ran off at the least sign of trouble. He'll make a fortune out of this war yet. You wait and see, and he won't spend it on that little scrap. Who knows? He might never come back. Especially if things are good in Canada. Likes his comforts, does Hermy. That's what attracted Sissy the first day. He had a good lifestyle. Knew how to give a girl a good time. Now if she had stayed at home and married a decent Irish Catholic boy poor Vicky wouldn't be on alien soil.'

'Vicky wouldn't exist,' Dad said, banging his newspaper – a sure sign that he disapproved of Gran's remarks.

'I'm only here for a few months. Until the war is over,' Vicky told me confidently.

She didn't eat much and we were sent to bed early. Her nose was as red as Rudolph's and her eyes watery from constantly crying to herself. I felt sorry for her but I got annoyed when she just wouldn't stop crying, no matter how much I tried to occupy and amuse her.

'Get her some decent clothes, Gertie.' Gran took down her pension book from its hidey-hole in the dresser. She counted out several pound notes and gave them to Mam.

'She needs new shoes. Her toes are squashed in those papery things she's wearing. She's so pale and delicate,' she tut-tutted to herself.

That meant another trip to Dublin but I wasn't looking forward to it. I wished Vicky had never come. She embarrassed me with her weeping and wailing. How could I let her play with my friends if she was going to snivel all the time and tell them she was going home? To make matters worse, Auntie Sissy wrote that the raids had finally started and with greater ferocity than was expected. She said in her letter:

There is no let up. We're being bombed night after night with every incendiary device available. No decent food either. I'm hiding under the bed most of the time or beneath the dining-room table. The real Battle of Britain has begun. Hitler ordered the Luftwaffe to destroy Fighter Command as an essential prelude to invasion. Goering sent four hundred bombers, heavily protected by a fighter escort, to raid London. We've no soap, tinned meat, biscuits. We expect the air raids to continue throughout the winter. Thank you for taking care of Vicky. It's such a relief to know she's safe.
Love Sissy

We took Vicky to McCullough's and Cassidy's and bought her summer dresses and a straw bonnet, socks and underwear and sandals. The weather was beautiful and Mam took us swimming at Sandycove. We bathed in near-warm waters and caught jellyfish in our buckets on the rocks. Vicky got stung by one.

'Bleedin' nerve that bloody jelly fish, biting me like that. It hurts, Auntie Gertie. It hurts.'

'Oh, shut your trap,' I hissed.

Mam put TCP on the red swollen patch but Vicky

insisted on going home and refused to go swimming again.

'The rotten bugger,' she called the jellyfish, to Mam's horror.

Her appearance began to improve with the good food and the light tan she acquired from all our walks along the pier. Gran marched us up and down the seafront, her knitting needles tucked under her arms, her fingers flying as fast as we walked. She made us accompany her into the church, on the way home to do the 'Stations'. There she continued to knit, her lips moving along with her needles. Her ball of wool was concealed in the pocket of her coat.

But as time went on Vicky seemed more lost and miserable than ever. The only time she was happy was when we were in the fields at the back of our house making daisy chains. We made necklaces, bracelets and floral wreaths for our hair. Vicky would sit patiently in the long grass pinching the green stems just down far enough to make a hole that wouldn't break. After a while we could thread the daisies inch by inch, fingers flying to create the most glamorous jewellery.

'When I grow up I'm going to be very rich and have lots and lots of gold jewellery with real diamonds and precious stones,' she said, her small hands working expertly as she spoke.

John was her other preoccupation.

She drooled admiringly over him and swivelled him

on her hip as she sang 'Hush little baby don't you cry' in a thin, sweet voice. John loved her. He would snuggle into her, his damp blond curls brushing her face, the crimp of his dummy still on his puckered lips.

'Poor little souls,' Gran would say, watching them finding comfort in one another.

We walked to the corner shop to get the messages for Mam.

'Would you like an ice-cream?'

Vicky seemed preoccupied with her own thoughts. 'Aniseed balls.' She perked up immediately.

'Twelve aniseed balls, please, five Woodbine and a turnover.'

Mr Dwyer wrapped the bread in thin brown paper. He placed the aniseed balls in a paper cone and gave the end a final twist to secure it. He made the best paper cones in Dun Laoghaire, it was said.

'You won't lose any of them.' He stretched his hand over the counter for the money.

Vicky wouldn't have them long enough to lose. She was addicted to their horrible taste. She had a trick of rolling them round her mouth until they turned from dull brown to a reddish colour; then she painted her lips with them, sucking them until they dissolved and only the tiny seed was left. It was the fabulous taste that she loved. She liked them because they were the best value for a penny too.

'The English have funny ways,' Jimmy Scanlon, who

had never met another English person in his life, remarked knowledgeably.

Vicky burst into tears.

'Shut up, Jimmy Scanlon,' I shouted and marched Vicky home.

I put the five loose cigarettes carefully into my pocket. Mam's rations for the day. Gran disapproved of her smoking and tried to make Mam feel embarrassed. She didn't say anything, just twitched her mouth, murmuring inwardly to herself as if she were praying, and shaking her head from side to side.

'Spit it out, Gran,' Mam would say occasionally when the tension got too much for her, but Gran would begin to leave the room, reminding Mam that her chest couldn't cope with the smoke.

As we walked home slowly the sun went in, the light faded and it began to rain. Pauline Byrne and Tess Mathews came running up behind us just as the heavy drops fell, wetting our thin summer frocks.

'Youse'll be drowned if youse go home. C'mon into our basement. We're starting a game of hospital,' Tess said.

'Her mother's out,' Pauline said. 'C'mon.'

May Tully was standing at a long scrubbed table in the middle of the big empty room of their disused basement.

'Hullo,' she said as I turned away.

'Aw c'mon, Lizzie. Play with us,' Tess pleaded.

'I'm the surgeon.' May Tully addressed Vicky with a

face that was ready to start a fight. She ignored me completely.

'I'd love to play. I'm going to be a doctor some day anyway.' Vicky's face was wreathed in smiles and I thought I'd better stay if it cheered her up.

'We're performing an operation. You, Jimmy, strip off and lie up on the table. I'm going to scrub up.'

Jimmy made for the door.

Our hands reached out and grabbed him and pulled off his shirt. He was forced to lie on the table while Tess, Pauline and Vicky held him down. I kept nicks on the door.

'It's only a game, coward.' May returned covered in a white sheet, a pair of old gardening gloves on her hands.

She began to make imaginary cuts on his chest with a pencil and he groaned at suitable intervals, because she was tickling him. May was obsessed with bodies and bloodthirsty rituals. She had a glazed sadistic look in her eyes as she diagnosed Jimmy.

'Appendix,' she pronounced. 'It's about to burst. We'll have to remove the patient's trousers. Knife, Nurse,' she called to Vicky.

Jimmy went to leap off the table but Vicky, with a piece of a rag tied around her mouth, pushed him and held him down with a strength that belied her skinny appearance.

'Hold still.' Her voice was muffled but insistent and he

57

shivered as she reached out to open the buttons of his worn brown corduroy pants. May covered his mouth with her dirty hand to stifle his screams. The others snorted with suppressed laughter as Jimmy's grimy underpants were revealed and examined closely by Vicky.

'Naked did you say, Doctor?' she asked, a gleam in her eye, her small face flushed with delight.

'Correct, Nurse.'

Jimmy wriggled and squirmed, choking his protest, but there was no stopping Vicky.

'I've seen lots of naked men,' she declared. 'In the war you know.'

'Oh la de da, I'm sure,' Tess mocked as Jimmy's pants fell to the floor.

'What's going on here?'

Mrs Mathews came thundering down the back stairs and into the room.

'I heard the commotion from upstairs. What in God's name are you doing lying there half naked, Jimmy Scanlon? In front of all these girls. You ought to be ashamed of yourself.'

Jimmy half rose from the table, purple with fear and embarrassment.

'Get dressed and get out of here. Go home all of you at once before I tell your mothers that you're up to no good.'

'We was having a game of hospitals, that's all,' chirped Vicky, looking as innocent as a baby.

'Oh, you was, was ye,' said Mrs Mathews, imitating Vicky's English accent.

Vicky spoke rapidly, tripping over her sentences, and skimming the tops of the words like stones skimming water. She hardly took a breath to let the meaning of what she was saying sink in.

'Well at least you're a nice polite child. Fancy these brats subjecting you to this sort of filth. Are you the little refugee?'

'Yes. I'm Vicky. Pleased to make your acquaintance.'

'Very pleased, I'm sure.' Mrs Mathews bowed. 'Now be off home with you. And Tess, you come with me. I want you upstairs at once.'

Tess, head bowed, followed her mother upstairs as we all filed out of the basement.

'I thought she was gone shoppin',' May shrugged. 'Good on you, Vicky. You impressed her with your limey accent and your manners. Got us off the hook.'

She gave Vicky a clap on the back and nearly sent her flying.

I could see the shape of things to come. If May liked Vicky she mightn't give me such a hard time of it any more. So Vicky had her usefulness. Coming over here might not have been such a bad idea after all.

The house was very quiet when we got home. Mam had a long sad face on her and Dad sat quietly reading.

'The cigarettes got squashed. Sorry.' I handed them over sheepishly.

'What kept you?' Mam was cross. 'You had no permission to stay out. Look at this mess. How can I smoke them?' She threw them on the table.

Vicky went to smooth them out. 'Where's Gran, Auntie Gertie?'

'She was very tired so I sent her to bed.'

'Can I go up to see her?'

'No. She's not feeling very well.'

It was unusual for Gran to be sick and the fact that Mam insisted that she stay in bed cast a gloomy shadow over the house.

She had caught a chill at mass one morning and couldn't shake it off. Now it seemed she might have developed pneumonia. Mam nursed her, making sure she was kept at an even temperature, and Vicky and I stole in to her often to see if there was anything she needed.

Doctor Pearson was sent for when there was no sign of Gran recovering. Her purple MG roared up the road announcing her arrival from the far end of Dun Laoghaire. Her face was heavily powdered and rouged, her vivid lipstick smudging her teeth. Her wide hat had a sweeping brim 'cocked to the Kildare side' and hid an abundance of yellow hair.

'That'll be seven and six,' she'd say to Mam each afternoon before making her pronouncements or writing a prescription. Then, adjusting her fox furs with a sweeping gesture, their dead glassy eyes staring out of her back, she would instruct Mam on how to treat Gran, while carefully pocketing the money.

Vicky and me would sit on the upper staircase watching the performance, miming her. She repeated the same thing every day.

'Plenty of fluids now. Hot drinks. Beef tea if she'll take it to build her up and chicken broth. Make sure she takes her medicine. Her chest is very weak.'

Gran was always tired and kept dozing off while Dad read her interesting snippets from the paper. Mam looked exhausted. Vicky and I took John for walks in his pram to give Mam and Karen a break. Vicky took charge of John on these walks. She strapped him carefully into his pram and secured his sun-hat on his head.

'Koochy koo,' she'd murmur along with other unintelligible little endearments, while we wheeled him round and round the square. John lay back gazing solemnly at nothing but seeming to understand every word she uttered. He never cried when we walked him. Just gurgled happily, his tiny face getting browner in the summer sun.

'How'll he ever talk proper?' Jimmy Scanlon said when he heard the special language Vicky reserved for the baby.

'How's chicky wicky today. Little scrumpy koochy koo,' he mimicked. 'What's all that mushy stuff you're sayin' to him anyways?'

'Mind your own business, don't mind mine. Kiss your

own sweetheart, don't kiss mine,' Vicky sang out, raising her head haughtily.

'Kiss your ass, you stuck up English snot,' he retorted. 'Why don't you go home and fight your own war?'

He walked off chanting, 'She who fights and runs away will live to fight another day.'

Jimmy hated Vicky since she had succeeded in undressing him. He never missed an opportunity to let her know.

'How's slimey limey?' he'd call out whenever he saw her, even in the distance.

To his great annoyance she ignored him.

May Tully came to look into the pram.

'So this is wonder boy?' she sneered.

John smiled a beatific smile as she tickled him.

'Why wonder boy?' Vicky's eyes widened.

''Cause everyone's wondering where his daddy is.'

My heart sank.

'Here, can I have a go?' She barged in front of me and elbowed Vicky out of the way, taking off with the pram, running down the road, the two of us tearing after her.

'Wait. He'll get sick.'

'He'll fall out.'

She wasn't listening. She turned into her own front garden and pushed the pram against the railings.

'Wait till me mother sees him. She's been dying to see who he looks like.'

She whipped him out of the pram and ran with him

up the steps and into her house, slamming the door before we reached it.

'Let us in,' Vicky screamed, banging loudly on the door. But there was no answer.

'What'll we do? We can't go home without him. Karen'll have a fit.'

I was frantic.

'Wait there.' Vicky ran down the steps and in through the open basement door. A few minutes later she came out the front door carefully carrying the bawling John down the steps.

'Hush now, Koochy. Don't cry. You're all right,' she said, fastening him into his pram. 'Let's go,' she ordered, marching the pram up home.

'What happened? What did Mrs Tully say?' I was breathless from running to keep up with her.

'She wasn't even in.'

'How did you get John back?'

'I told May I'd knock her bleedin' block off if she ever so much as looked at this pram or this baby ever again.'

'You said that to May Tully? Vicky, you're brave.'

Suddenly an ambulance came tearing up the road, siren going full blast. It stopped outside our house. Mam was standing at the open door, tears running down her face. We stood gaping as the stretcher was carried into the house, Mam following the ambulance men. They carried Gran out on the stretcher and into the waiting ambulance. A small knot of neighbours had gathered while they were inside. Gran looked tiny and very frail and when I ran to kiss her goodbye someone pushed me back.

'I could have minded her.' Mam was wringing her hands. 'I told the doctor but she said she needed hospitalisation. I failed her. I failed the poor old woman.'

'That's nonsense,' Karen said, taking John out of his pram and carrying him into the kitchen.

We huddled together around the range after the ambulance drove off, thinking our own thoughts and feeling miserable. Even Vicky, who had known Gran for only a short time, was heartbroken. Dad came home for tea.

'If Doctor Pearson thinks she should be there then that's where she should be.' He looked sad though.

When he took me to see her a few days later I was shocked to see her lying there with needles in her arm and tubes stuck up her nose. Mam's eyes were red rimmed.

'You can only stay a minute, Lizzie.'

Gran kept dozing off. The doctor came in to check her.

'She's recovering. She's lucky she's so healthy,' he said in a stiff formal voice. 'She'll have to take things easy when she goes home. She'll feel worn out for a while.'

I never wanted Gran to wear out. She was the centre of our home. She gave it permanence. I picked up her roughened hand and held it tightly and wished she would talk to me. Even a caustic remark from her sharp tongue would have been welcome.

Next time I saw her she was sitting up in bed.

'Oh, Gran. You look so much better.' I hugged her.

Her white hair was combed and pinned in a neat bun. Her eyes had their old sparkle back.

'I hope you prayed for me, Lizzie?'

'I did, Gran. Every single night.'

'Keep up the prayers and I'll be home before you know it. It's quite comfortable here really,' she conceded, secure in the knowledge that she would soon be going home.

I decided to pray for Paul's safe return, seeing as my prayers for Gran were answered so speedily. But each time I tried to imagine his face I couldn't. He was weightless in my mind, his features vague, and the more I prayed for him the more distant he became. I decided not to say this to Karen. Paul's name was never mentioned any more and I wondered if she might forget all about him in time.

Mrs Keogh

It was soon after Gran came home from hospital that Mrs Keogh came to work for us on a weekly basis. She was a sharp-faced little woman with dangling earrings and a black felt hat that she wore all the time. A hint of orange shone through her black hair, at least the bit that revealed itself under her hat. She dispensed advice and kindness with the same force of character she used to get her work done.

Her family had lived in Dun Laoghaire for generations and considered themselves part of the town. In her eyes they were equivalent in stature to the army and the navy because they fought in the troubles of 1916 and had the medals and the pensions to prove it. They were the establishment. Their whole lives were devoted to maintaining it, no matter what the demands and pressures were. They were ready to serve their country yet again should the need arise. One of her sons was ensconced in the Curragh in Kildare at that very moment, waiting to take up arms against the enemy.

'If Hitler dares enter British soil my mum'll be ready

with all the ammunition she's making out of old railings and kettles,' said Vicky. 'They even took the gates off Hyde Park and sent them to the factory to be made into ammunition. You should see the size of Hyde Park, Lizzie. Cor blimey, your park would fit into one corner.'

'You're glad enough of our park to play in, 'specially sliding down the steps of the bandstand. You've slid down them that many times you've put a shine on them.'

'Now now, girls. Birds in their little nests must agree.' Mrs Keogh spat that little saying of hers out regularly, reminding us of the 'Birds' Nest' in York Road, a Protestant orphanage our teacher constantly threatened us with for the least misdemeanour.

I hated the mention of it and could hardly bear to pass by it. It was a long dismal three-storey building with ivy-clad walls. No children were ever seen entering or leaving it and the sound of children's voices never emitted from it either.

'They get swallowed up in a huge tunnel once they get inside,' Jimmy Scanlon told us with conviction.

He said his mother told him and she swore she'd send him there and pretend he was an orphan if he didn't learn his lessons.

Mrs Keogh began her day with a 'drop of tea to work up her strength'. This strength was crucial for her morning's work and her long conversations with Mam about her latest family problems. Mam liked her and, now that Gran was confined to bed for the moment, she was glad of the chat.

One day towards the end of the summer she came as usual and, adjusting her hat, sat down to have a cup of tea with Mam. She looked very distressed.

'He's gone,' she said. 'Just upped and went. Not a word.' She was breathless with rage.

'Who? Who's gone, Mrs Keogh?' Mam was puzzled.

'Mr Keogh. My husband. Gone off with Madge Ryan. You know, that slut from the dirty end. The slovenly one with the dyed blonde hair who neglected her family. Not fit to wipe my shoes and he's left me for her.' Her voice rose and her nose quivered with indignation.

We maintained a respectful silence in the background so that Mam wouldn't suddenly become aware of our presence and throw us out of the kitchen before we could hear the rest of the story.

'I'm so sorry,' was all Mam could think of to say.

She knew that Mrs Keogh's husband was always on the move. He was a bit of a dandy, dressed up in cream trousers and sandals, for ever combing his Brylcreamed hair.

'He'll get enough of her. I warned him about her before. But would he listen?'

'I'm sure he'll come to his senses and come home soon,' Mam said.

'I'm sure I don't want him if he does. Not after being with that trollop.' She spat out the word trollop as if it left her with a bad taste in her mouth.

Mrs Keogh saw the black side of everything, Gran said. Now this Madge was the blackest she'd ever seen.

Mam looked at the clock and Mrs Keogh, clucking like a hen, went to get the cleaning equipment.

'Let 'em rot in hell. I'm not having him back,' she said before she went to do the polishing. She worked automatically and between washing, ironing, polishing and carpet sweeping she was kept busy until lunchtime, fitting in odd jobs along the way. With Gran sick, it was Dad's idea to get help. Although he would never call either Vicky or the baby a burden, there was still a lot of extra work. We never realised how much Gran got through in the day until she became ill.

That morning Mrs Keogh's face was an angry red and her earrings swung violently as she put the full force of her rage into her work. 'No good will come of it, mark my words. Deceitful git.' She was talking to herself.

'Where did they go?' I only asked because I didn't want her to feel deserted. Mam had gone up to Gran's room on some pretext.

'Who knows? Maybe to England. Took the boat, I wouldn't wonder. He's been seeing quite a lot of her.'

I watched her work, her hat bobbing up and down as she polished and felt the weight of the world on her scraggy shoulders. She took the rugs out to beat across the railings, looking off down the road, her thoughts miles away. Probably on the boat to England.

'Don't worry, Mrs Keogh,' I said, dragging the rugs

back in. 'I bet Mr Keogh will soon be back under your sparkling roof.'

She wasn't listening.

'Blame meself I do. Should have seen it coming. But of course the wife's always last to know. Wait till I get my hands on him.'

Tears glistened in her eyes.

'Listen, Lizzie. You're too young to know about matters like this. Your mam'll kill me for discussing me matrimonials with a little one like you. Now don't say a word to no one.' I waited curiously as her voice hushed to almost a whisper. 'I might have been a bit unfair . . .'

Mam came downstairs.

'Lizzie, make yourself useful. Give little John a bath to help Karen.'

I finished feeding John, soothed him, burped him and got the blue basin ready, filling it with water from the big bath. He gurgled, splashed and kicked contentedly while I soaped his little body and washed his hair.

'Aren't you the grandest baby in Ireland?' I wrapped him up in a big fleecy towel and took him back to Karen.

'Mrs Keogh is very upset,' I told her while she dressed John in his navy and white sailor suit.

'What's wrong with her now?'

'Oh nothing. I'm not sure.'

'She's always moaning about something. How that husband of hers puts up with her I'll never know.'

Karen brushed John's hair into neat shiny curls.

'There's nothing in this world more beautiful than a newly bathed baby. I could just eat him,' she said, hugging her little son tightly. 'He's getting like his daddy already, and I'll tell you something, Lizzie Doyle, I'll never give up hope that Paul will turn up. It keeps me going.'

I didn't dare tell her what May Tully had said. That would really have upset her.

There was a lot of work with John. Between bottles, burpings, cooings and changing nappies we were kept very busy. Vicky wrote less and less to Auntie Sissy. She didn't boast about London and the enormous size of everything compared to Dun Laoghaire or even Dublin any more. She hardly mentioned the war except when someone passed a remark about it and she felt the need to better it or correct them, as she considered herself an authority on that subject. She'd dried her eyes long ago.

When May Tully and the gang decided to stage a play, Vicky found where her true talent lay.

They let her play the part of Snow White because she had a pert, pretty face, and a not-bad voice. That's what May said but I suspected she wanted to be on the right side of Vicky. I was stage manager and it was my job to open and close the curtains. As Vicky pointed out, seeing my disappointment, it was an important job because the timing was crucial. The blankets pegged on a clothesline swayed in the breeze and flapped open in the centre when the wind rose or a bulge appeared as members of the cast arranged the props. The rehearsals took place in May's back garden on fine days and in her basement on wet ones. May was director and producer of course, so she got to give out the parts. Everyone wanted to be in it, even Jimmy Scanlon. He brought a couple of his gang 'to even out the numbers', he said, but we knew it was for protection. Two of them were given parts as dwarfs because they weren't very tall. We ransacked our mothers' wardrobes, attics and anywhere we could find costumes. Doctor Pearson gave Vicky some long ornamental dresses in vivid lilacs and greens, costume jewellery and old hats, because only Vicky had the nerve to ask her. Two weeks before the end of the summer holidays we performed the play. The whole terrace was invited: adults one shilling, children sixpence.

Everyone came. The blankets quivered and strained with the shifting and moving behind the scenes and finally I unpegged them slowly, my fingers barely showing above the clothesline to reveal the makeshift wooden stage. The audience applauded, deadening the loud whispers from the prompters. Vicky appeared in a white lacy blouse and flowing green skirt tucked in pleats into her waist, her face painted in May Tully's pancake stick, her lips a gaudy red. The dwarfs were a bit tall, but what they gained in stature they lacked in stage presence and constantly forgot their lines. May prompted them. Her stage whispers reverberated around the gardens and everyone sniggered.

Even Mrs Keogh came to cheer us on, her hat bobbing up and down as she sang along with us: 'Heigh ho, heigh ho, it's off to work we go'.

'It's off to England her oul' fella went,' Mrs Tully said under her breath. 'Doesn't seem to be missin' him much. If you ask me she's glad to see the back of him.'

'Nobody asked you.' Mam gave her such a sharp look that Mrs Tully nearly fell off the wall.

Mam rarely lost her dignity but she hated gossip just for its own sake.

'Sorry, I'm sure. No offence. Mustn't offend the Doyles. They're gentlefolk, of course.'

'Shhh,' someone hissed as the blankets quivered back into place and the stage emptied for the interval. The audience ignored the pushing and shoving and hushing that went on behind the scenes and Mam ignored Mrs Tully and invited all the cast home for lemonade and plain biscuits after the show. May was allowed into our house to count the money they had taken at the gate.

It amounted to three pounds and was donated to our school for the children's needs. Everyone cheered and clapped except Vicky who called May 'bossy boots' and May retaliated by saying that she wouldn't have had to be bossy if Vicky wasn't such a 'stupid eejit'. Vicky gave her a dig in the ribs and Mam collared her and told her if she was a bit more submissive she'd be better off.

The nuns who ran the school were grateful. They took wonderful care of the Catholic orphans and protected them fiercely from the outside world. We were the outside world mostly and if we were caught saying one unkind word to an orphan we got into real trouble. Sometimes we even got a slap from Mother Gonzaga's bamboo cane.

I dreaded returning to school but the fact that Vicky would be with me was a consolation. She was making her mark, afraid of no one, least of all May Tully.

'They've had no holiday, Bill,' Mam said to Dad the day after the play. 'They'll be back at school soon.'

'Karen and the baby could do with a break too. We could do with a break ourselves. It's been a busy time,' Dad agreed and immediately sat down to write to Uncle Mike, his brother who lived in Limerick.

'Mike will only be too glad to have them and while they're away it'll give you a rest too, Gertie. You look pale.'

Dad had got a new job as manager of the Home and Colonial, a large grocery shop in the town. The money was good and he loved the work. Mrs Keogh's wages were half a crown a morning and he urged Mam to get her in an extra day if she felt like it. He would have money for our holiday too, he said, while balancing his accounts in the corner of the sitting-room.

Karen was first in the taxi with John. He was dressed in his blue coat and hat, dangling on her knee. Vicky and I sat on either side of her, Dad in front with Mr Trainer, the taxi driver.

It took nearly an hour to reach Kingsbridge Station. Gran gave us pocket money, slipping the shiny coins through her thin, veined fingers. The pound notes she kept for Karen. 'Children must be respectful at all times to their relatives and have respect for their native place,' she told Vicky, who didn't consider County Limerick native to her. She'd never even heard of it. But her eyes shone as we squeezed into the train and found the most comfortable seats. Dad waved as the train chugged out of the station leaving behind the sprawling city. As it gathered speed, the houses thinned out in ragged disarray and soon we found ourselves surrounded by green fields and hedgerows.

'Bet you don't have fields in London like this?' I was confident in that knowledge because even I had never seen so much open space.

She rolled her eyes and screwed up her mouth in disbelief, conceding without words her amazement at the surrounding beauty. The weather improved as the train raced on into the countryside. The sun shone, casting the trees in silver-white sunlight as we passed through Tipperary. The Galtee mountains rose out of all the green, their blue granite peaks streaked with purple. Everywhere sparkled. Haycocks dotted the fields in various shades of yellowy-beige, some with their tops covered. Crops made lacy green patterns like embroidery on a cushion.

Vicky held the baby while Karen doled out the sandwiches and lemonade. Afterwards she fed John his bottle and he went to sleep, the swaying of the train rocking him gently from side to side. We read our comics when we got tired of looking out the window. Vicky had introduced me to *School Friend* and *School Girl's Own Library* which she'd brought with her. I read them over and over again.

Uncle Mike was waiting for us. He was a big man, with a peaked cap and a sunny disposition. He bore a vague resemblance to Dad and none at all to Gran.

'Isn't it welcome ye are,' he said to Karen, lifting her suitcase like a feather into the back of his trap as she thanked him for having us to stay.

'Your Auntie Peggy's waiting. She's everything ready. This must be Lizzie. Be the hokey you've grown a lot since I saw you last.'

'I'm ten and a half.'

'I'm Vicky.' Vicky put herself forward, hand outstretched.

'Is that a fact now. I'd niver have guessed with that hoity-toity accent of yours. But you're a grand little girl. The image of your mother.'

'Gran says she's more like . . .'

Karen poked me in the ribs. Uncle Mike hoisted himself up into his trap. His stomach hung over his trousers like a sack of potatoes and swayed from side to side to the rhythm of the horse's hooves.

'Faith, ye brought the weather with ye. Grand weather for savin' the hay.'

Vicky looked at me and sniggered.

'It ain't possible to carry weather around, Uncle Mike . . .'

But he was chatting to Karen who sat up beside him while we were jostled from side to side behind them, our backs supported against our luggage.

Auntie Peggy was at the back door of the whitewashed farmhouse waiting to greet us, the smell of sizzling rashers wafting through the door.

'Ye're welcome, children.' She extended her arms in an all-encompassing embrace. 'You must be tired. Look at the lovely baba. Who's he like at all?'

'He's like my husband,' Karen said, her voice dropping on the word husband.

'Sure, 'twas a terrible sad thing that happened to your husband.' Auntie Peggy led us into her gleaming kitchen.

A fire burned in the range and, shutting the door on the cool evening, she sat us down. In one corner there was a table laden with home-baked bread and cakes such as we hadn't seen for years in Dublin. A big dresser stood at the far end, with blue willow-pattern plates and knick-knacks.

Tall, with shining coppery hair, Auntie Peggy stood smiling down at us, her sleeves rolled up, and then removing her apron she led us across the stone-flagged kitchen to the scrubbed table.

'Mike, take their coats and put their things in the spare room. Ye must be starvin'. Now Karen you must niver give up hope. Niver. Always believe that your man is coming back from the war and he will.'

From the moment she uttered those words Karen was a changed person. She smiled brightly and Auntie Peggy and herself became the best of friends with an understanding between them that Karen had found nowhere else.

Karen had been to Uncle Mike's several times when she was growing up because Dad drove there often in his own car. But that was either when I was a baby or before I was born.

We woke up early next morning in the big feather bed shared by Vicky and me, with the birds singing gaily to a clear blue sky. Uncle Mike came in from the farmyard clanging the milk buckets on his way to the 'separating parlour'.

'We're early risers here.' Auntie Peggy was frying slivers of bacon on a black frying pan and cutting hunks of soda bread.

Vicky plastered her bread in thick yellow butter and began eating ravenously.

'It's the country air. Gives you an appetite. Now, Vicky, how many rashers? Will you have an egg? Fried bread, sausages? Little mite wants proper feeding after the tragedy she's been through.'

I discovered early on that food was the antidote to

everything in that house. It cured all ills, healed all wounds, even Karen's broken heart. It was lucky for them that they weren't rationed. Tom, their son, came in for his breakfast. He was tall and gangly and stared at us as if he'd never seen girls before.

'You're townies,' he teased. 'Bet you niver milked a cow in your lives.'

'So?' Vicky said. 'Bet you was never in a war like me. In the Blitz I was. Bet you was never in London.'

'Who'd ever want to be in London when you can milk the cows here in the fresh air?'

He winked at me.

'Now stop your teasin', Tom, and eat your breakfast.'

Auntie Peggy placed an enormous plate of food before him and he ate rapidly, devouring every morsel.

'Gives you an appetite, milking, does it?' Vicky asked.

'Certainly does. You can do it tomorrow. I'll teach you to milk Betsy. Lizzie can have Daisy. She's quiet. Doesn't kick like Betsy.'

'Thanks a bleedin' lot.'

Karen came in to quieten Vicky while Tom roared with laughter.

'We'll knock it out of her, don't fret,' he said. 'Introduce her to a nice young farmer. Then she'll know all about work, and forget all about posh London.'

'I hate farmers,' Vicky shouted and stormed off after Uncle Mike.

I stayed to clear the table and make myself useful. They

had the new plumbing installed and were very proud of the hot and cold water that came out of the shiny new taps.

'Until a couple of months ago we had to go to the well for every drop. That's a mile away. Course we had the rainwater in the barrel. I still keep that for washin' the clothes. Softens 'em.'

Auntie Peggy kept her house spotless. We dried the dishes in the whitened flour bags; the same flour bags that were bleached and sewn together to make sheets.

Vicky scattered meal to the hens and sent them flying in all directions.

'Don't frighten them.' Tom took the bucket from her and showed her how to throw the feed gently and we watched them furiously pecking. His large ears were wrapped in cabbage leaves to protect them from the sun. He looked hideous. I don't know if I was more scared of him or the hens.

'They don't lay if they're frightened,' he told us, running ahead to show us all the places where they laid their eggs. 'The haggard, the special nests, the loft, the hayrick.'

We were taken on a tour of the farm and given our duties. Collecting the eggs was my favourite one. I never brought in less than twelve eggs each day to Auntie Peggy.

One day on my return I heard Karen telling Auntie Peggy that she'd no money and, with the future so uncertain, she didn't know what she was going to do.

'What about finishin' your nursin'?' Auntie Peggy asked. She'd been a nurse herself before she married Uncle Mike.

'Well, with the baby I'm not sure.' Karen was hesitant. 'I don't want to impose any more on Mam and Dad. They've been so good to me already. But they're not getting any younger and I can see it's a struggle.' She clutched John tightly to her. 'I couldn't bear being parted from John.' Her voice was shaky and she buried her face in his hair to hide her tears.

It never occurred to me that Karen might need money. Suddenly I was upset at the anxiety in her voice.

'I've everything provided for me now but I can't impose on them much longer . . .'

I crept away, knowing that the conversation wasn't for my ears but was confidential between herself and Auntie Peggy.

There was a lovely parlour in Uncle Mike's house with a carpet and heavy, comfortable chairs. The piano had brass candleholders on each side that shook slightly when Auntie Peggy played and sang for visitors.

Oh the days of the Kerry dances,
Oh the tune that the pipers played.

Her voice rang out and Uncle Mike sat back smoking his pipe, enjoying his wife's accomplishments.

All the relations were gathered in our honour and I met people I recognised from Karen's wedding and the christening.

Uncle Mike took all the children off to the crossroads for a céilí and my cousin Patrick danced a hornpipe, a row of medals pinned on his chest, the buckles of his shoes glinting in the evening sun.

'Came first in the Feis,' his mother said, puffing out her chest.

'Don't care what he came first in, he's stupid looking,' Vicky whispered to me. 'Dances like a stick. Doesn't move his body or his arms. All rigid-like.'

'Irish dancing's like that. You're not allowed move your body and you must keep your hands by your sides.'

'Stuff that for a lark! I go to ballet in London. Much more graceful.'

I tried to picture Patrick doing ballet in his hornpipe shoes and tittered, making Vicky snigger. Karen beckoned us to leave the room. We were glad to escape and took John for a walk up and down while people all around us danced together.

We helped with the baking. Gran had taught me the basic method so I was able to roll out pastry.

'You're a useful child.' Auntie Peggy smiled at me, her hair in a roll around her head in the fashion of the day, her eyes dancing green lights.

I was growing very fond of her.

She cooked bacon for dinner nearly every day with cabbage and floury potatoes, which we smothered in the rich yellowy butter churned in the morning before breakfast.

Auntie Peggy made the butter. She separated the milk first and churned the cream in a huge wooden churn. She used two wooden laths to pat it into shape.

Uncle Mike told us stories about the family in the evenings and played the old gramophone. He had a collection of 78s. Count John McCormack singing 'Jeanie with the Light Brown Hair' was his very favourite and 'I Hear You Calling Me' came a close second.

'Your Uncle Tommy joined the British Army and disgraced the family. He daren't show his face in the parish, or the county for that matter. Gran never forgave him or spoke to him since.'

'Where is he now?'

'In America somewhere. Making a fortune I suppose.'

'Paul is American,' Karen said. 'Who knows, maybe they'll come across each other yet.'

Uncle Mike had definite views about everything and didn't mind airing them.

We played with Tom in the hayrick, sliding down the hay, and chasing one another. He always won because he was older than us and stronger. He was fourteen and their only child. Vicky said he was spoilt.

'Takes one to know one,' was Tom's quick retort.

We walked endless dusty lanes, called 'boreens', and picked apples from the old grey trees in the orchard. We heaped them into crates, checked them and Uncle Mike graded them. Cox's Pippins, Orange Pippins, Bramleys.

We got paid one pound each for this job because

Uncle Mike was making a fortune sending them to Dublin to the market. There were so few imports on account of the war and with the scarcity of fruit my uncle was laughing all the way to the bank. That's what Tom said and sure enough Uncle Mike laughed all the time.

'Ireland is economically self-sufficient,' Tom told us. 'The farmers are very proud of that fact.'

'Thanks to Mr de Valera,' Uncle Mike added. 'The incentive comes from him.' He had the same dogged devotion to de Valera as his mother. Gran must have instilled it in him from a very early age.

Uncle Mike took us to the market on the last day of our stay. Stalls were laid out up and down the main street of Oula, the nearest town. People crossed and recrossed, buying and bargaining, and by eleven o'clock the town was crowded.

Milk, butter, eggs, bacon, even salted fish were all in plentiful supply. Everything that was either rationed or prohibitively priced at home.

'If we'd brought bigger suitcases,' Vicky said, 'we could take home some of this lot and make a bundle selling it on the black market.'

'Have you no heart, Vicky? Do you think of anything else besides money?'

'Not much,' she replied. 'Anyway what's wrong with that?'

Uncle Mike sold his produce and gave us money for

sweets. We bought sticks of pink and white rock with 'Welcome to Ballybunion' written on them, though we had no idea where Ballybunion was.

'Gran has a bunion on her toe,' I told Vicky.

'They've hardly christened some place after it,' she laughed, taking a bite of 'Gran's bunion'.

'Delicious,' was her verdict.

Of course, she bought her supply of aniseed balls. The shop was tiny and filled with every kind of sweet. The woman serving from behind the counter squinted out from thick glasses as she wrapped the sweets in copy-book paper. Uncle Mike took us to the pub. We had lemonade while he drank a pint.

'Only the one, mind. Peggy doesn't like me drinkin' on market day. She doesn't like me drinkin' any day.' He laughed heartily, introducing us to all his friends. 'These are the toffs down from the big smoke, and this little one comes all the way from London. Could you credit that?'

Everyone gaped at Vicky. They didn't meet many people from London, especially people who had had experience of the war at first hand as she had. She played it for all it was worth, telling them horrific stories about the Blitz.

'We hid under the bed when the incendiaries were dropping down, one after the other, setting fire to the houses.'

'Was your house set on fire?' a small boy asked, his eyes, wide as saucers, fixed on her face.

'We was lucky – we escaped, but only by inches. When we woke up one morning the whole street was gone up as far up as our house. There was a huge crater where the houses had been right up to our front door.'

The wild look in her eyes and her whiny cockney accent intrigued her audience. They rushed to buy her more lemonade and sweet cake and begged her to tell them more but Uncle Mike declared that it was time to go.

'There's nothing to look forward to now,' Vicky moaned that night. 'Just going home and back to school.'

May Tully and the Gang

We left early for school. Not because we wanted to be the first in but because we wanted to avoid May Tully and the gang. Early morning was a quiet time for reflection, especially this particular morning. Even Vicky, who liked to chat a lot, respected this.

That first morning as we kissed Mam and Gran goodbye our hearts were heavy. The lapse of time until the next holiday seemed interminable. So many things had happened since the outbreak of the war and the first working day of the 'Emergency' had been declared.

'No reason for panic', the news bulletins had said but we had plenty of reasons. We were a country apart for the first time in seven hundred years. The coal, electricity and gas were in short supply, so we couldn't heat ourselves sufficiently and the winters were freezing. We had our family problems too. All arising from the war.

The 'glimmer man' came regularly to check our gas jets. Mrs Tully didn't like the glimmer man 'coming in to lay his hands on my jets to see if they're still warm'.

I could hear their distant voices down the corridor of my memory as I trudged back to school. I could hear Karen's incessant crying when the telegram arrived just after John's christening and remembered her crushed spirit. If the war was the 'non-event' everyone said it was, why had it played havoc with our lives and affected all our family? Poor Auntie Sissy slaving in the munitions factory, not really welcome since she'd married Hermy. Vicky plunged into an unknown world; which she was taking to, mind you, like a duck takes to water. Dad and Mam had the dubious benefit of two extra mouths to feed on rations and poor Gran had collapsed from the stress and strain of it all.

By the end of the summer holidays tea and sugar were really scarce, fruit unobtainable, and many other items a luxury.

'Well, we had the holiday. Plenty of food there and as much as we could carry home,' Vicky reminisced.

Uncle Mike had laden us down with parcels of eggs, butter, cheese, bacon and apples. He'd have given us more if we could have carried it. He also sent Auntie Sissy an indirect invitation home, even though he hadn't really spoken to her since her marriage.

'I hate this war,' I said aloud.

'It has its good side. I mean, you got me 'ere wiv you.' Vicky thought she was indispensable but my fear was that if she stayed too long she would be.

'I suppose,' I conceded.

I wished Karen had heard from Paul and that Gran was fully recovered and then I remembered what Gran said about being grateful for what we had. I was thankful for Gran, Mam and Dad, Karen and John, and Vicky too. Thankful that Dad had a job and that we had enough, which was a lot more than many people had.

As we turned the corner and tried to by-pass the tight knot of school children clumped together outside, whispering and nodding towards Vicky, I wished with all my heart that there was no such place as school and that I could go to Birmingham to work in a munitions factory.

We sat next to one another in the high-ceilinged school room and waited for Miss King, the teacher. The mumble of voices of children coming in and May Tully writing with squeaky chalk on the blackboard in front of us 'Welcome back, Miss King' made me feel sick.

The wooden double desks with holes for inkwells seated two. Vicky sat next to me undaunted by her status as a new pupil, a foreign one at that. She weathered the stares by smiling genially back. Staring was something you knew not to do in our school if you'd any sense. Because if you stared at a person, even if you just looked longer than a split second, a piercing cry would emit from the victim: 'Are ye lookin' whatya lookin' at?' This embarrassed the starer in the extreme if they had the sensitivity to become embarrassed. Not everyone did.

Miss King marched in, hair in a net, eyes glittering behind rimless glasses, lips squeezed tight. She looked smaller, more shrivelled, since we saw her last. The holidays had done her no good at all.

'Open a window,' she sniffed. 'There's a musty smell.'

May, who sat up at the front, ran for the window rod to open the high, many-paned windows. In spite of them the room was dark, the smell of disinfectant concealing the less savoury taint of chalk and unlearned lessons, cruelty and insensitivity.

'You're in Fifth class now girls.'

Miss King had a habit of stating the obvious.

'I see we have a new pupil. Stand up. Name?'

Vicky stood up.

'Victoria, Miss.'

'Victoria whom?' Miss King placed great emphasis on the whom.

'Victoria Rosenblume, Miss.'

There was a guffaw of a laugh silenced by Miss King's steely gaze around the room. 'I gave no one permission to laugh. You must be our little friend from London.' She was thawing out slightly.

'That's right, Miss. I was in the war.'

Eyes were thrown up to heaven and 'Here we go again' came in a hoarse whisper from the back of the classroom.

'Silence,' roared Miss King. 'Where did you get the name Victoria, dear?' Miss King asked, entering Vicky's name in her roll book.

'My mum christened me Victoria 'cause she met my dad outside Victoria Station.'

'So you mean to tell me you're called after a station?'

More stifled laughter, with Miss King thumping on the table for silence.

'No, Miss. Just Victoria, Vicky for short.'

'I see. In this country we tend to give our children the names of the saints, like Brigid, Mary, Ann, Elizabeth,' her eyes roamed the room.

'Elizabeth's the name of one of our princesses, Miss. She's not called after a saint. They don't have no saints in England.'

'Are you a Catholic, Vict . . . Vicky?'

'Yes, Miss. I was christened.'

'Well then, sit down and we'll begin. It's time you were all acquainted with the present circumstances of our country. You're old enough to know about the economy.'

'Or lack of it.'

'Who said that?'

Tess rose. 'My dad's gone to England to work, Miss King. There's no work here. He calls this country the island of scants and collars. Politicians laying down the law and no work.'

'I'm sorry to hear that, Tess. But there is an Emergency. Although we are not actively participating in the war there is genuine hardship. Wages are at a standstill and incomes frozen. However, the economy is ticking over.

The politicians can alleviate the problems caused by outside influences. Mr Lemass is doing his best. There is genuine deprivation but it could be worse. We could be suffering like Victoria's parents. Emigration is the only solution. Britain is anxious for people to work her industries. A lot of farmers are gone to work in factories in Birmingham. At least we should be grateful to Britain for the work.'

'God save the King.'

'Who said that? Stand up at once.'

Silence.

'I'll find out and if I don't I'll punish you all.'

More silence. Miss King knew when she was defeated.

'Now let us consider the British map.' She rolled down the enormous, age-worn map and began listing the countries in Europe involved in the war. 'Neutrality is something not to boast about but to be grateful for.'

Vicky helped her along, describing the starving children in rags standing outside piles of rubble, once their homes.

'The children in Britain are not all as lucky as Vicky here. They are deprived and although we are not prepared to lift a finger to help them we will pray for them, night and day.'

'Pray that they don't start coming over here in droves for safety. One Vicky is enough,' Pauline whispered across the desks to me.

By the time the bell clanged for break we were saturated in history about the 'European War, and Hitler'. Nobody had any sympathy for these invisible, faceless people Miss King was talking about. Her reference to their starvation brought on real hunger pangs and we finished for the morning with a decade of the rosary. I closed my eyes and concentrated on Paul for the duration of the prayers. After break we had arithmetic, which was even more boring. Then we played hopscotch and ate our lunch of jam sandwiches. We drank water from the tap in the yard when we got thirsty. At half past two we walked home, tired and hungry after the day.

One day followed another. Karen walked John for miles in his pram. She held her arms out to grab him in a rapturous hug when he took his first unsteady steps, pride shining through her tears.

'It's lovely to see her so happy with John,' said Gran.

'Don't cod yourself. Her heart is breaking.' Dad's eyes misted over, concern for his beloved Karen etched in every crease of his face.

Mam made our winter coats, staying up late to have them ready for the really cold weather. The trees turned beautiful shades of gold, burnished copper and dark red. The leaves began to fall. We kicked the heaped pile of dry leaves in varying stages of decaying orange, squelching them underfoot on wet days.

Mrs Keogh went to England, some said in search of her missing husband, but Mam said to get work. Gran was her old sprightly self, buzzing around again.

Karen suddenly announced that she was returning to England to finish her nursing and search for Paul. She must have consulted Mam and Dad because they weren't surprised.

'I have to go, Lizzie, and do something positive. I'm dying inside, here,' she pointed to her heart.

That was true. She was a shadow of her old self and even John didn't give her the joy she'd once known.

'What about John? Won't you miss him?' I fought to hide the tears.

'Of course I'll miss him. But I'm burning up. If you could only feel what I'm feeling. At least there I'll be useful. Even if I can't find Paul, I won't feel I've deserted him.'

I didn't understand. But Mam and Dad did.

'She'll be burning on the outside if she goes to London.' Vicky put into words everybody's fears.

The war had escalated and London was under siege, but there was no keeping Karen at home any longer. She packed her bags and Dad and I took her to the mailboat.

Life continued, with the street getting greyer as the winter progressed. Yet the shabby houses on that occasionally sunlit street came alive with our games. We played Cowboys and Indians. A game reserved for winter.

'Hands up. Come out with your hands up or I'll shoot.'

I crouched behind the gable wall at the far end of the terrace and Pete Scanlon, Jimmy's older brother, called my name.

'Lizzie, quick. C'mon. Follow me. I'll get you out safely. Quick.'

I ran with him along by the low wall, his face intent as we ran, his hand extended to catch mine and help me up through the skylight of his granny's house and on to the roof. We ran along the parapet, the wind blowing back my hair. We laughed together high above the street. We were safe from the baddies. I followed him as, agile and catlike, he leapt from one jutting roof to another, his imaginary hills. His corduroy jacket hung loose, his cowboy hat was pushed back off his forehead, his freckled face framed by a thatch of sandy hair.

'Watch out. Oul' Mrs Tully's roof is rotten. It wouldn't do to fall down on top of her. Give her a heart attack it would.'

We laughed and laughed, his eyes bright and animated. Vicky was with the baddies and they searched long into the evening before they found us. I felt important, with Pete Scanlon. I was one of the real gang.

Then there were the rehearsals for the Christmas pantomime in our garage; Pete doing his impersonations of Jimmy O'Dea, his wiry body swaggering around dressed up as Biddy Mulligan, swaying to the rhythm of

'Biddy Mulligan the Pride of the Coombe', his mobile face ecstatic as he strutted up and down.

His voice, still unformed, sang out strong and true, holding promise of something richer and fuller.

'He's talented. Has a great future,' the judge said when he won the talent contest in The Workman's Club in Dun Laoghaire. Proudly we stood beside him, his mother and me. Vicky and the rest of the gang were cheering from the back of the hall. That talent contest was the first one I ever attended and it was so exciting I couldn't wait for the next one.

Just before Christmas Uncle Tommy in Boston, whom we hadn't heard from in years, sent us a parcel. It was a huge brown paper parcel tied up with lots of white string and glued together here and there with red wax.

There were pairs and pairs of the new nylons for Mam, fancy picture books, lacy underwear and a sort of fur coat.

'Nothing useful,' Gran said, turning her nose up at it all.

Mam made me wear the coat, telling me it was lovely and warm. But I hated it. Its brown moth-eaten fur hung loosely around me. I can still see the hostile faces of the rest of the gang as we walked home from school.

Pete Scanlon came to my rescue, defending me staunchly against their wounding taunts and jeers.

'Leave her alone, lads,' he shouted but the taunts became more vicious.

'Did your granny leave it in her will?' they laughed, eyeing the mottled fur that almost touched my ankles.

'No. Her father went to the North Pole to shoot polar bears. This is one of the skins.'

One of them pushed me.

That did it. Suddenly Pete rounded on them, taking them on single-handed. Grabbing and punching, arms flailing, legs kicking, he waded into them. Then everyone was fighting. Raggy and defiant kids, our friends turned enemies. Suddenly this was no game.

It took old Batty Brown on the corner to stop the fight.

'Get home with ye outa that,' he roared, separating us all.

Pete walked home with us. We were silent. I felt isolated in my shame.

'Why did you do it?' I asked him as we stood at our gate.

'They had no right to make fun of you like that.'

His voice was croaky and strange with pent-up emotion and unshed tears. Then he looked down at me and suddenly he burst out laughing, defusing the tension.

'Anyway, I think it's a terrific coat,' he said before he sauntered off home.

Pete left school quite suddenly. He was older than us. About fifteen or sixteen. I argued with him but he wouldn't change his mind.

'Working hard at the books is not for me. I'm sick of the deprivation and poverty. I want to make money.'

'You have to stay at school and pass exams.'

'I don't agree. I can't take it seriously.'

We were all walking along the Pier, watching the harbour lights reflected on the water. Everyone was arguing and nobody was listening to anyone else's point of view.

'Lizzie, I want to make something of myself.'

I understood because I wanted to leave school too. But there was no chance of that so I didn't mention it.

Already tall for his age, he was decisive and certain to make a future for himself. He stood there, arms akimbo, explaining to me, an awkward, skinny child, why he had to go. All the time I listened I was wishing he would put his arms around me.

'We'll miss you.' I was remembering the day we played cops and robbers in his granny's basement. The gang tearing through it, firing imaginary shots as they went. His father, coming home drunk, catching us redhanded as we raised the roof in his granny's absence.

'Get out, ye skunk,' he had roared at Pete, delivering him a well-aimed kick, as Pete tried unsuccessfully to duck past him.

I brought him home, pleading with Mam to let him sleep on the sofa. I couldn't leave him with that forlorn and haunted look about him. It was the final turning point for me. He would never be just an ordinary friend again, he would always be special.

'Your father's cruel.' I was indignant.

'He doesn't mean it. It's the drink.'

The day he left home I was allowed to walk with him to the mailboat. With his guitar slung nonchalantly over his shoulder, he waved goodbye in a deliberately careless gesture. I stood there, my heart sinking, already missing my pal.

As I faced home alone my despair was mirrored in the wet street. Shielding my eyes from the rain I thought of his mother missing him as much as we missed Karen. The icy wind whipped around me and I cursed Dun Laoghaire and the mailboat that slipped sneakily between the outstretched arms of the harbour taking with it chunks of my life. Until Pete let me join his gang, knowing my frustration with May Tully, I had hated boys and avoided them. But he was different.

There were letters from Karen to all of us.

London, December 1940

Dear Mam,

How are you all and how's my darling baby? I miss him so much but I'm settling in well. The patients on my ward are female, of various nationalities. Some are very ill. One poor old lady from Yugoslavia calls me endlessly on any pretext just to talk. She's so lonely. It's a twenty-eight bed ward so I can't give her the attention I would like to. Matron hauled me over the coals for being 'sentimental'.

We've started lectures and I haven't forgotten much of what I learned already. But I'll have to study hard to pass the exams. We're expected to get it done in our own time. The subjects are hygiene, anatomy and physiology. Luckily our tutor is nice.

We aren't allowed into the heart of London yet. But I hope to go soon when things quieten down.

In spite of the workload, I'm happy. I have begun bombarding the War Office for any information about Paul. I have also written to his commanding officer.

Please write soon,

All my love,

Karen. xx

Dear Gran,

Thank you for your letter and the pound note you so kindly enclosed. I will buy the silk stockings when I get up to the West End. I may be able to send some home. Our uniform stockings are black and thick. We work at such a terrific pace that my feet are swollen. There is never enough time to get all the jobs done, which is a good thing for me. I had too much time to think at home. I'm known as a 'dogsbody' still because the work I do is basic. I can't wait to get into second year. Matron lectures a lot about etiquette. We may not speak to the doctors or address senior nurses unless they speak to us first. Difficult to remember in a crisis. This week I'm on morgue duty and I can tell you it's not pleasant. The morgue is the busiest place here at the moment.

Glad to hear your rheumatism is improving.

All my love,

Karen. x

Dear Lizzie,

Thank you for taking care of John for me. I miss him so much I can't tell you. But he's a lot safer with you. A little bird told me you cried when I left. What about the special chocolates I promised if you didn't cry? Now you must keep your side of the bargain because I won't forget mine.

We had lectures on various parts of the body today. Bones were drawn on the blackboard and there is a skeleton in the corner of the classroom named Fred. We love him dearly. We bandage one another for practice and do 'dressings'.

When next I write I'll be able to tell you what the West End is really like. Meanwhile think about Christmas. It's not far away and I'll try to get home to see you all. Love and kisses to you and John.

Your loving sister,

Karen

Dear Dad,

In spite of the alerts we walk through the park and try to fool ourselves that we aren't scared. We're more scared of the loud wolf whistles and the staring eyes of the strangers.

The queues are long outside the shops. Everything is scarce.

The ravages of war are being felt. We went to the Hammersmith Palais. It was full of soldiers and naval officers talking in strange languages. My heart broke thinking of Paul. I even found myself scanning the crowd. How ridiculous.

The sirens are terrifying and we rush to makeshift air raid shelters in the basement when they start up. The shelters are shored up with steel girders and sandbags. They're cold and damp, and the atmosphere is pessimistic. There is a feeling that we'll never survive the Nazi onslaught and if we do we'll be in a sorry state.

I'm doing everything in my power to try to get information about Paul. My colleagues here think there isn't a hope. That I'm wasting my time. But I'll never give up hope. It's all I have. I love you, Dad. Pray for me.

Karen

The next time Karen wrote it was after the Battle of Dunkirk.

London, June 1941

Dear Family,
I want you to know that I'm all right.

It's been chaotic here since the Army and Red Cross lorries rolled in from Maidstone, one after another, with the battle victims. We assembled government-issue bedding and found extra pyjamas and sheets. There was uproar trying to accommodate the hundreds of patients, some very badly burnt. Everyone is irritable from lack of sleep. But the surgeons are doing a great job. I help prepare saline drips and spend most of the time coating the patients in gentian violet for their burns. They're only boys most of them. Love the chat and attention, lying there inert, or groaning in pain. There are no meal breaks while this crisis is going on. Just coffee and snacks. Trench foot is the biggest problem. Socks are embedded in the men's feet. Luckily this sad cargo of injured soldiers is beginning to rally. They love a cigarette when they're not drugged with morphine. It seems now that they jumped out of the boats into the sea which was a mass of flames. The best of the army they are too, by all accounts. We use large quantities of wintergreen and iodine.

The acrid smell in the wards is dreadful. Mavis, who is now much more experienced than me, keeps fainting in the sluice. I keep thinking of Paul and hope he's not lying injured somewhere like this. Then I hope he is, because that would mean he's alive.

The armada of small ships lifted the army off the beaches. 'We will fight them on the beaches,' Churchill said on the radio yesterday. How right he was.

All my love to my darling John.

K

PS Write and tell me every little detail about his progress.

Gran wrote back:

Karen, You shouldn't be there. I'm worried about you. Are you sure you're all right? I have a terrible premonition that you are being bombed mercilessly. Let me know. Write immediately. How can you sleep with all that racket going on over your head? I hear they're spending all their time sweeping up shattered glass and replacing it with wood. There won't be a window left in London. Keep your head down. When will you get sense and come home? I suppose it will have to end some time. John's making good progress. Write.

Your ever loving Gran

Our fears for Karen became constant. According to Auntie Sissy's letters to Vicky, the dust of the bombed and devastated buildings swirled in the air. The smell of charred wood was everywhere and dangerous buildings had to be pulled down.

Vicky was now part of the family. So, when Dad told her that Auntie Sissy couldn't come as planned for Christmas, it didn't seem to worry her.

'I wasn't really expecting her,' she confided to me.

'Aren't you lonely any more?'

'Not really. Anyway, Mum's work's more important. If it weren't for her we wouldn't be winning the war.'

I wasn't certain who was winning the war but I didn't have the unshakeable confidence in England that Vicky had. But then I wasn't British nor was I an authority on the war like Vicky. She was nothing less than heroic in her willingness to sacrifice her parents for the cause and I was full of admiration for her. She rarely mentioned her dad and he wrote only once. He was working in Toronto, making parachutes out of raincoat material and making himself a fortune into the bargain. But he did send her a doll for Christmas. She walked and talked and had silver-blonde hair. Vicky christened her 'Camilla' after her best friend at home in London. She was a very pretty doll with her own wardrobe of the finest and latest fashions. We didn't use her much in our games because she was heavy and awkward. Her clothes were too good to peel on and off all the time. She was more of an ornament residing in a corner of the sitting-room and performing for visitors, striding, one leg positioned stiffly in front of the other at the press of a button. Vicky boasted to the whole neighbourhood about Camilla, so for ages afterwards there was a procession of callers enquiring to have a look at her. Vicky wanted to charge 'viewing fees' but Mam wouldn't hear of it.

'You'll get us a bad name,' she told her crossly.

Vicky showed her off, marching her up and down in different outfits, but she preferred to play with my doll, Annie.

That was one talent Vicky and May Tully had in common. A talent for making money. Always dreaming up new schemes, never missing an opportunity. Mam was getting annoyed.

'Vicky has Gran bled white, getting money from her at every hand's turn,' she told Dad.

I had visions of Gran lying on the floor with Vicky struggling to get her purse while she bled unceasingly from the punches Vicky delivered. But Vicky's methods were more subtle than that. It was the 'little girl lost' approach that did the trick. Any mention of Auntie Sissy, or a crocodile tear, or a letter from London with a mention of the war, sent Gran running for her purse. A letter from Auntie Sissy was worth at least a half crown, or a half dollar as Vicky lovingly referred to them. She stashed them away in a drawer 'for rainy days', only using pennies for aniseed balls. If the war continued much longer she was going to be worth a fortune like her dad.

Karen couldn't come home for Christmas and neither could Pete Scanlon. He wrote to his mother to tell her that he was 'joining up' and she nearly had a fit.

Life took on a slower pace in our house. Time was measured in letters from Karen more than by calendar dates and we continued to mind John, who was growing bigger and bouncier with each day. Karen sent him a brown teddy bear and Gran knit him a whole new outfit in lemon yellow. She said she was tired of knitting in blue.

But John was really Mam's baby now. She devoted most of her time to wheeling him to the shops and taking him into the ten o'clock mass. He began to think of her as his mother and she was delighted with his possessiveness.

'Poor little orphan,' May Tully said.

'What do you mean? He's not an orphan.' I was very indignant.

'Well his daddy is supposed to be missing and now his mammy's gone, so what else is he only an orphan?'

★ ★ ★

Christmas was made cheerful by John, who got presents from Santa and was awed by the glittering tinsel we hung from the ceiling. Dad brought home a turkey and Gran cooked it until its skin turned a crisp goldeny brown. We said grace before our dinner and prayed for Karen, who seemed to be missing every Christmas now.

Mam always invited someone less fortunate than ourselves to share the meal and this time it was Mrs Keogh, home from England for a few days. She sat in Karen's place, her new 'pudding bowl' hat bobbing in delight.

'Any word of your husband?' I waited until Mam and Gran were busy at the range.

'Don't mention him to me. I hear they've moved on. It seems she might be in the family . . .'

Voices drowned her words as heavy plates of food were passed around and I was left to guess what Mrs Keogh was going to say. I couldn't.

May devised a new game early in the spring. It was called 'ghost trains'. Her mother was gone to the country to mind May's sick granny and her father was out at work all day. May was desperate to make money. She had started hanging around with older girls and became increasingly concerned about her appearance, rolling her hair up in pipe cleaners for half an hour at a time so that it curled at the ends. Nylon stockings were hard to get and she couldn't afford them anyway so she bought a bottle of brown liquid stuff and rubbed it into her legs, then got Vicky to draw a pencil line straight up the middle of the back of her legs in an imitation seam.

'Make sure it's straight,' she'd shout at Vicky, who licked the eyebrow pencil furiously to get the line as dark as possible. Gran said May looked like a tart and advised Vicky strongly to keep her distance. It was too late. Vicky and herself were becoming inseparable, their love of dressing up in adult clothes and making money being their common denominators. Common was a word Gran used often to describe May.

The cost of a ride in the 'ghost trains' was a penny a go. We all queued up outside her house and waited our turn.

As soon as I handed over my penny I was blindfolded and led to a waiting 'train', which was May's young brother's bockety old pram. From then on I was at her mercy because she was the train driver. She raced the pram through the hall screeching 'choo choo, choo, choo' whenever it occurred to her and ran me into one of the empty rooms off the hall. The air was dank with the smell of toilets. One of the shutters flew open as May drove past and a ghost covered in a sheet jumped down on top of me almost wrenching off my neck as well as my blindfold.

Then the 'train' took off again with a screech from the background and on to another shutter in another smelly room. It flew open when May gave the command and something cold and wet was flung into my face. Lights flashed and I was wheeled rapidly into the next room, where I was surrounded by ghosts in white sheets all chanting and pulling at the pram until it toppled over and I fell out screaming. May bundled me back in and rushed me outside again into the welcome fresh air. It only took about five minutes in all but it was exciting and exhausting for May. Vicky took turns at 'driving the train' and she was merciless, toppling the customers out every few minutes. She broke all the speed limits.

We all had several turns and, although the queue went halfway down the street and the takings were good, May's profit wasn't as high as she'd have liked. She had to pay her 'ghosts' and the sound effects operator, who was Vicky.

May now began to wear lipstick and powder and scent called 'Ashes of Roses'. She told Vicky in secret that she had a boyfriend.

I laughed when I first heard it but she did seem to cause some anguish among the older boys. She hung around corners, looking up and down the road, always ready for a chat with a fellow who might be passing. She went for solitary walks down the back lane in the hope of meeting some of the lads. She had no magical qualities yet she had the boys chasing after her. They all wanted to be her friend and seemed to act funny, saying stupid things in her presence. She had a trick with her eyes that made them nervous and excited. I was left out of all this because Vicky and herself decided that I was too young and impressionable to join in their 'secrets'.

'May Tully has a natural inclination to gravitate towards the lower elements,' Mam said disapprovingly.

Vicky bounced out and slammed the door with elaborate insolence.

'She eats like a pig too. May is a terrible influence,' Mam told Dad, who tut-tutted and retreated behind a dignified silence.

May and Vicky huddled together in our coach house giggling and laughing. I wasn't allowed in because they were talking about adult things. Yet it was my 'den' originally.

The rules for Vicky and me differed because Gran made them up as she went along, the emphasis being her pity for Vicky.

'Vicky has her wrapped around her little finger,' Mam said, noticing that I was more and more on my own.

I blew my breath on to the vestibule door before polishing it and rubbed and rubbed in ever-increasing circles, wishing Mrs Keogh would come back just to hear her chatter. I was desperate for someone to talk to, someone like Mrs Keogh who would talk endlessly and require no input from me. I secretly yearned for Pete Scanlon. John couldn't talk to me and Gran read more and did her knitting. She was delaying time, slowing it down, waiting to hear from Karen, waiting for the war to come to an end. Waiting, waiting, endless waiting.

Vicky asked to sit beside May Tully at school with the excuse of getting help with her Irish. May, being the eldest in the class, was good at her lessons, which seemed to excuse her boisterous behaviour. She was protective towards Vicky. They walked home together ahead of me, ignoring me, sniggering at the boys. I hated them and wished the war was over so that Vicky would go home. No such luck.

Gran knitted me a hat, mittens and scarf to match my coat for my birthday, as the weather was still cold. I had refused to wear the fur thing long ago after the incident with the gang and reverted to the brown coat Mam had made for me. Wrapped up warm, I walked through the lane alone, avoiding the cracks, in case I married the devil. Tiny buds began to appear on the bare branches and lambs were born in the cropless fields. May and Vicky had merged with the rest of the gang, united in their combined 'secrets'. They laughed and jeered at my new rig-out or the way I walked, whether I was in front of them or behind them. I hated Vicky for her desertion of me. In the yard in school she yelled at me and threw stones that ricocheted off the wall next to my ear. She chased me around and around the playground with a terrifying old bone, shouting that it was part of the skeleton of a German bomber pilot who'd lost his way. She wouldn't walk home with me any more. Shrieking with glee she raced after the boys, who scattered in awe and mock fear.

'None of your lip', was May Tully's favourite expression and she used it liberally whenever anyone spoke to her. Outside the school gate she changed personality. She was permanently giving boys the eye and by now she had well and truly initiated Vicky in her new 'direct technique' approach, which involved insinuating herself into their conversations as they gathered at corners. The others laughed at the pair of them and their total abandonment of inhibition as they approached the 'lads'.

Now Gran was furious with Vicky for associating with May and her 'lavatory jokes'.

'She'd go with a pair of trousers on a clothesline,' she told Vicky. 'You watch out for yourself my girl. We don't want another scandal in the family.'

'What scandal?' Vicky was all agog but Mam shut Gran up with one of her withering looks.

'I speak as I find,' Gran sniffed.

'We know,' Mam retorted.

When May was in good humour she entertained us with graphic descriptions of the more biological mechanisms of her body. She showed off marks inflicted in passionate moments. The chain of purplish-yellow love bites around her neck were her pride and joy. She wore them like a badge of honour, pointing out the fact that certain parts of the body were 'errogunous zones'. Vicky said she read that in a book she found in the library. May went around with the fat sleek air of a cat who got all the cream.

I felt the same hatred and anger for May and Vicky that Karen felt for the Germans who robbed her of her husband. But I didn't let on. It would only have upset Gran.

Vicky quite soon lost interest. Initiating herself in the wonders of the male species must have proved boring. 'I don't really want to be beautiful,' she told Gran. 'I prefer to be clever and you can't be both.'

'Course you can,' said doting Gran. 'You are both beautiful and clever. You're my granddaughter aren't you?'

Vicky preened herself visibly. I stayed in doing some of the chores Mrs Keogh did, afraid the others would notice that I was always alone. I polished the furniture with beeswax, and helped measure fruit and chop up nuts and cherries for Gran's birthday cake. It was to be a surprise and Dad had got the fruit through a friend of his in the trade. Hanging out the washing was still my favourite job. Squeezing the clothes through the mangle and pegging them close together to save space and pegs. Often they blew stiff in the cold air.

'Why aren't you playing with Vicky any more?'

Gran had sharp powers of observation. She knew there was something wrong and set about putting it right. Only she miscalculated the situation.

'I hope you are kind to that poor child, Lizzie. She's separated from her parents. Think of her pain and sorrow.

You were always a kind child, so now go and play with her and keep her cheerful.'

'I hate her,' I exploded. 'She's so evil that everyone hates her, except you. The only reason you don't hate her is because she's an evacuee and different from us.'

Vicky walked into the room.

I doubled my fists and scowled at her.

'I hate you too,' she roared. 'So there. You're a tell-tattling pig.' She bloated her jaws and blew an enormous raspberry at me.

I went to grab her but Gran slid between us.

'Cut that out,' she screeched.

In spite of being thin and small, Gran could be amazingly strong and energetic. She darted in and out between us, pushing at one or other of us, trying to keep us apart. I managed to hit Vicky in spite of Gran's intervention.

Her face crumpled up and she burst into tears.

'Lizzie, you ought to be ashamed of yourself. Apologise at once.'

'No,' I screamed. 'She should apologise to me for being so horrible.'

Gran sat Vicky down and put her arm around her.

'If you were my little girl,' she scowled at me, 'I'd punish you good and proper.'

'What would you do?' I simpered, pretending not to be afraid, but my heart was thumping in my chest.

'I'd, I'd . . .'

'What's going on here?' Mam said, coming into the kitchen with a pile of ironing.

Vicky jumped up out of her chair and ran upstairs. We could hear a door slam.

'Oh God. She's locked herself in the toilet.'

'Lavatory,' Mam corrected but Gran was gone, calling, 'Vicky, Vicky.'

'Now you've done it,' Mam said. 'Can you not control that temper of yours?'

'Gran's little pet. She can't do anything wrong. And she's horrible. If Gran only knew the things she does.'

'Calm down and listen. Gran feels protective towards Vicky and under the circumstances you can't blame her. But you're my little girl and I know what's going on. Just put up with her for a bit longer. She'll settle down again and meantime I'll have a talk with her.'

I unclenched my fists and burst into tears.

'I wish I'd never set eyes on her,' I said.

'No you don't. You'll look back some day over the years and you'll be glad you helped Vicky. Think of what might have happened to her in London.'

'I suppose so,' I conceded.

'Now give me a hand with these sheets and make it up with her and Gran. Life is very short you know.' We folded the sheets while the iron heated against the range. Gran returned.

'I'm sorry, Gran,' I whispered.

'What did you say?' She bent her ear close to my mouth.

'I'm sorry,' I repeated.

'Good. Now you and Vicky better make it up. I gave her a good talking to so I expect to see an improvement in the behaviour of both of you.'

Gran's face was pinched and pale during her little speech and I was truly sorry for upsetting her.

'I love you, Gran,' I said grabbing her by her thin shoulders.

'That's enough of that. Now wipe your eyes and be off with you.' She pushed me away but I knew she was pleased.

Gran was engrossed in the wireless and Vicky had disappeared.

'Gran, I can't find Vicky anywhere.'

'Shh . . . They've dropped bombs on the North Strand. Gertie, come quick, listen. The war's started here too.'

It was the last day of May, a week after Gran's birthday, when bombs were dropped on the North Strand, killing twenty-eight people and injuring many more.

Gran tuned into the wireless constantly to hear the news. The Germans mistook the North Strand for the English coast, perhaps Liverpool. The survivors from the terraced houses devastated by the bomb were moved to temporary accommodation, their loved ones lost to them for ever.

'I thought your mother was going to stop the enemy

getting in here?' I forgot my promise to be nice to Vicky.

'Mind your own business,' came the curt reply.

Vicky was the only one who was happy with the bombings in Ireland because anything that postponed her return to London was welcome. Local men with pickaxes and shovels came to dig up the rubble and horse-drawn carts took the debris away.

Peat smoke hung heavy in the air in the city as the walls of turf in the Phoenix Park diminished. Tram bells clanged and horses' hooves clippety-clopped over the cobblestones as order was restored to the shocked people of Dublin.

Children ran barefoot in the street still. Poverty was prevalent.

Vicky was right. The Germans were definitely coming. German bombers ditched here and there throughout the country and were taken to the prison camp in the Curragh for the duration of the war.

'Poor souls,' Gran said, forgetting that they were the enemy. The crowd who'd done away with Paul. Or maybe he'd ditched somewhere in some country and was in a safe prison. I began to pray that he was. If Paul were alive it would make such a difference. Even though I had only met him once, on Karen's wedding day, the impact he'd made on all our lives was incredible.

Karen wrote to say that Paul's diaries had been given to her by the authorities. They had been smuggled out of a

Gestapo jail in France. They were delivered by Intelligence, who warned Karen that they were not proof in themselves that he was still alive. Anything could happen to a prisoner in a Gestapo prison, they said. But Karen's delight was evident in her letter home to us. She felt that her solitary and relentless search for him had not been in vain.

As far as she was concerned, the diaries were proof positive that Paul was alive. Gran believed otherwise.

'If the Gerries have him, that's the end of him.'

Karen sent us copies of the diaries.

Paul

Extracts from Paul's war diaries.

Dark moon.
Way high up in the sky
Tell me why oh tell me why you've lost your splendour.

The sky was black as pitch over the peaceful countryside. A deceptive peace reigned. We were flying in low formation. Over one hundred of us. It was our first mission out. A carefully planned mission that we had trained for since our arrival on British soil and possibly since I joined the United States Air Force. It was also a mission that had to work.

Flying above the earth was my favourite place to be. I felt in charge of every situation. In the pilot seat with one eye on the instrument panel and the other on the repeating compass, I was in charge. My pilot's mate sat silently beside me. Alert. We were flying in unison over the English countryside and out towards the horizon. The bomber aimer sat behind, with the rear gunner, the navigator, and flight engineer. The crack gunner sat up in front. Seven of us all bound for Germany.

We were at war.

I combed the sky, relaxed into my seat and steered my course toward the North Sea.

I had to be calm. My men were nervous and inexperienced. My training was over. This was for real. I was one of the first American recruits, because when they said war had broken out in Europe that's where I wanted to be. I had always wanted to be a fighter pilot. Our training in England was inadequate because we were restricted to night-time flying to avoid detection.

The enemy was waiting 'at the gate' we were told from strategic positions. Waiting for the Lancasters. We weren't all ready for them. The bomber crew were suffering from lack of sleep, making them short-tempered and jumpy. They blamed everything on the weather, the crew, the plane. The formation separated. We were on our own, heading for our separate destination.

I told myself it was a job and should be treated as such. Our instructions had been issued. We were to bomb dockyards, ships, submarines and oil tankers. All in the day's work of a fighter.

Up until now I had no responsibility for anyone else. Team work was different. Gone was a happy, carefree existence. The casualties were too high for the job to be fun and now I had six other lives in my hands. I closed my mind.

We ran our engines together, evenly, until each plane was at zero six hundred feet, then the brakes were released and with powerful acceleration we were airborne, climbing. Wheels up, flaps up, we had cruising power. I kept my oxygen mask on. I knew every inch of the cockpit so I never had to look for the controls during a flight.

We raided Hamburg and Cologne, destroying industrial areas. We were briefed between bombings while the bombs were being loaded on to the aircraft. Often we were ready for take-off when a red light would signal the cancellation of a raid and we would return to wait around the crew room. We got nervous and jumpy when the waiting was too long. We played cards and cracked foolish jokes, hiding our fear deep down, well below the surface.

We flew out night after night attacking Hamburg or Dusseldorf on bright starlit nights, flying low to find the aiming points. The full moon often cast us into a near-daylight dangerous brightness. Avoiding collision with each other was of primary importance.

I wanted to get home, and in good shape too. That was an obsession, your face before me constantly. I thought of you during the missions and lived for the day we would be together again.

We were sitting in the mess playing cards when word came that you had given birth to our baby son. I was waiting for orders to scramble. We had finished a massive raid the previous night, and seen German bombers fall out of the sky like flies. I felt deliriously happy and sick. Sick that I couldn't touch a drop of drink to celebrate the birth of my son and sick from the killings that I realised I was becoming immune to. Carnage and wreckage everywhere and I was just sick of it.

Our flying skills were improving. My goggles were heavy and the heavy-duty gloves hindered the handling of the controls and gun buttons. We flew out in foggy conditions. I owned the sky the night you gave birth. Well I had a beautiful wife and now a son. Everything. I'd show those German bastards who was calling the tune. I spotted a German bomber and the temptation was too much. I chased him but from nowhere came the roar of stukas. Diving, I was caught, the bullets ricocheting off my tail as the stukas opened up. We hadn't a chance. They tore the tail and ripped off the wing.

I remember that I was floating high with no knowledge of where I was. I wasn't going to ditch in the Channel because land came towards me. The fog gave way to misty rain and I rolled over into the earth.

On my feet, I rolled up my parachute, hid it and ran for cover in the nearby woods. I had to find out where I was and try to make it back to England somehow. If I was going to bump into anybody, I prayed to God that it would be a French man. A friendly one preferably.

I released the harness of my parachute, unscrewed the valve of the Mae West and was free with nothing worse than scratches and bruises. I slept that night under a tree in an orchard. A sleep peppered with hideous dreams. Horrific sounds of diving stukas exploding gunfire that rent the sky. I dreamt of you then and prayed that I would see you again soon.

I don't know if you will ever read this Karen but I'm hopeful that you will and that if anything happens to me you will understand better from reading it. I was captured and taken to the main Gestapo headquarters in Paris for questioning. I knew I was doomed.

In a makeshift office I was questioned by a man whose steely eyes bore into me as he rasped questions at me. Then I was cross-examined. There was an English interpreter there. I told them nothing. Just about you and the new baby. They weren't interested in my life history and became impatient. The part I had played in the war so far was their concern. They wanted to know about my 'secret missions'. On and on they probed. Their loathing for me and my uniform becoming more obvious with each question. I devised a system to stop myself thinking. I concentrated on you at home, waiting for me. I would get home. I would see you again. We would be together. The officer lost his temper with me. He slapped my face until I was dizzy and promised more severe punishment if I wasn't forthcoming with the information. He didn't have to tell me. I knew what he meant. I had heard the stories about these places too. I longed to sleep and eventually I was put in a dark cell in the basement. The lock turned on the barred door.

The damp mattress stinks of urine. They won't kill me if they think I will talk.

For a week now I have been interrogated by a fanatical officer who keeps losing his temper when I don't answer him. Sometimes he explodes with fury. Here in the cell there is no one to see or hear my cries and I can call your name aloud. It makes me feel nearer to you. The cold, damp meals are brought by guards. One of them isn't bad. He gives me a cigarette in the evening and escorts me on my walks. He gave me the paper and pen in return for my flick knife which I'd managed to keep hidden. Who knows, he may use it on me yet but that's a chance I've got to take. Writing to you is bringing you nearer all the time. It keeps me from cracking up in this monotonous existence. They shout 'schnell, schnell', pushing me to and fro with rifle butts. I am developing a fever. Last night I was delirious. I thought I was at home with you. I could even see you holding the baby. I was so happy, I would gladly stay delirious if it meant that I could be with you, if only in my dreams. Remember I love you and our child, though I have never seen him. I love you with all my heart.

My cell is bare and damp. Only a mattress and a calendar. I got it from the guard who's friendly. I tick off the days. I wait for 'lights out' then I take out my pencil and pad from under the mattress. The light from the panel over the door gives me enough light to write because I've become so used to the dark. The mattress is horsehair and hard. When I get home we'll start again. A real family this time. We'll buy a cottage and have a spare room. Space. You never have enough space. The worst thing, worse than a hard mattress, is sleeping alone. I imagine holding you in my arms, which makes my desire for you almost unbearable. We'll decorate the cottage with pretty wallpaper and curtains to match. I'll do the decorating myself. Did I tell you I'm pretty handy with a paint brush? You never got a chance to find that out, did you?

The atmosphere here is tense. Fights break out easily and you can hear them screaming or crying out in the distance. I put my hands over my ears and think about us. Soon it'll be Christmas again and I have no present for you. Next Christmas I'll make sure to be with you.

We'll decorate the tree together and make the day really special. We'll stroll through the park in the snow and, when we come home frozen with the cold, we'll drink each other's health and cook dinner.

I'll cook the turkey. I always helped Mom with the turkey at Thanksgiving. I can cook most dishes if they're not too difficult. Then I'll give you your present and watch the glow of happiness on your face.

If I was a bird I could escape. There's a tiny hole in the high window just in front of the iron bar. Enough for a bird to get through and fly out. Fly up into the air away from here. I could fly straight to you and land beside you as if I'd never left you.

If only you could write to me, tell me what you're doing. Just the ordinary things, like holding the baby, shopping. If I were there I could help mind him, play with him, Cowboys and Indians, soldiers. I have a box of tin soldiers back home for him. I hope you are safely at home with your family by now and not worrying too much about me. The nights are so cold that I worry about you and the baby being cold somewhere too. I am gripped by a feeling of helplessness because I'm deprived of the responsibility of taking care of you both. So guilt creeps in with the other emotions. If only we'd been given a chance. We could have lived lightly without extravagance and have been so happy.

This evening I was given more exercise. I believe that is a good sign. They are watching my health.

The food is dreadful but I eat it just to stay alive. People look at us through the railings as we march around in circles. We are not allowed to talk. So I don't know if there is anyone else here from England or the States. I can't see anyone who looks English but then none of us look like ourselves.

We'll grow vegetables. I'll dig out a plot specially for the growing of tomatoes and cabbage and green beans. I love vegetables and the baby will benefit from them. We'll drive in the countryside. I'll buy a convertible and take you out into the open spaces. We'll go to the sea. Sea that goes on and on into infinity. We'll swim and take our son for a paddle. Let the water suck in around his feet as the tide retreats, pulling the tiny pebbles back into the sea with such ferocity that they sound like the clang of chains and the bolting of doors being quickly locked. I'll never take open spaces for granted again. We'll eat our picnic in the dry warm sand dunes. We'll have visitors sometimes. If you want, I'll cook the meal.

They've given me a coarse blanket because I have a cough that won't go away. They gave me medicine but didn't trust me to take only one measure at a time so it's taken away after each dose.

Paul's diaries ended abruptly here. What had happened to him? Why had he stopped writing? We were afraid to even think about it.

Auntie Sissy wrote to say that she'd changed jobs and was an air raid warden. She felt it was her duty to help protect the people against the enemy. She worked among the dust and bombed buildings, reduced to rubble, piled high over basements. Buildings held together with timber beams. She said she was hoping to be nominated for a George Cross for extreme heroism among the civilian population. She double-checked people in every street she was in charge of.

'London is tired and shaken, the squares grimy and

black with soot and ash. The houses are raining dust and mortar if shaken.'

Vicky was most impressed by her news. So was I.

'Imagine a George Cross, Gran. Won't you be proud?'

Gran shrugged her indifference.

'Imagine Mum in a uniform, all important. How brave!'

Vicky mooned over the letter for ages.

'Stubborn, more like,' Gran said. 'Sissy always liked to be where the action was. How she married such a dead opposite as Hermy I'll never know.'

Vicky obviously took after her mother.

Pete Scanlon returned home for a holiday. Although he'd lied about his age, he was still too young to enlist.

He had broadened considerably since I'd last seen him. Still dressed in an exaggerated cowboy style, he was wide shouldered and lean hipped. There was something different about him. Not only had he grown stronger but he was more confident too. His smooth sandy hair fell over one eye and he raked it back continuously with his hand.

'When'll I see you?' he called to me from where he was standing by the railing with a group of lads. I was sitting on the steps dangling John on my knee and waved casually back, but my heart leaped in my ribcage. He grinned his lopsided grin and his blue eyes shone with mischief.

But I didn't see him and wondered where he was. He

didn't call and I decided to play the waiting game. Anyway, I didn't really want to see him until I'd been to the hairdresser. Mam had become friendly with the new hairdresser who'd opened over Burton's and was up-to-date on the latest styles, having just returned from a training course in London. Mam was treating me to a hairstyle for my birthday.

Hermy

One day a dark-coated man wearing a black hat appeared at our front gate, hesitated before opening it, then mounted the steps and rang the bell. I was watching from the bay window and ran to open the door.

'Is your mamma home?' He removed his hat politely before stepping inside.

His voice had a slight foreign inflection. There was something mysterious and dignified about him.

'I'll get her.'

'It's Hermy,' Gran said coming into the hall. 'How did you get here Hermy?' Her voice was direct and not as friendly as I would have wished. I cringed with embarrassment but Uncle Hermy didn't seem to mind. He smiled broadly. A smile that gave his faded handsomeness a more youthful expression.

'I got a boat to Liverpool. Terrible times, terrible times.' He shook his head sadly. 'That mumser Hitler has a lot to pay for.'

'Why are you here?' Gran's directness gave me a sinking

feeling for Hermy somewhere in the pit of my stomach.

'I'll put the kettle on.' I retreated down the hall.

'How did you make out in Canada?' Gran was asking when I returned, but if Uncle Hermy had made a fortune he gave no indication of it.

'The air here is wonderful,' is what he said. 'So crisp.'

Vicky had approached him shyly and when he proffered his face for a kiss she seemed to shrink from him. But it didn't put him off.

'You look wonderful, my *liebling*, a little fatter perhaps than I remember.'

Vicky's face turned scarlet but she said nothing. Although she had filled out she wasn't fat. I knew from her self-improving rituals with May Tully that the very word upset her. Uncle Hermy continued to smile at her, blissfully unaware of his *faux pas*.

It was after grace as we sat down to eat that he dropped his bombshell.

'I'm taking Vicky back to Canada with me,' he told us all and looked at Vicky as if he were handing her the moon.

Now Vicky's personal war was over. The war that had been such a waiting period for her too. Waiting to go back home, to make up for lost time, to grow up, to make money.

'Sissy sent me a telegram to say you were dying of pneumonia. So I came as quickly as I could,' Hermy told Gran.

Gran was astounded.

'I'm hale an' hearty, thank you very much. Sissy always exaggerated. Strikes me she wants to shift her responsibilities elsewhere, so she can become a war hero.'

Gran was more irascible since her illness but nonetheless a new admiration shone in her eyes for Uncle Hermy. He was becoming a hero in an entirely different way. By showing us all that he cared so much for his daughter.

He came to the school to thank the nuns for teaching Vicky and for their interest and kindness to her, even though he hadn't mentioned when they would be leaving. He stood, hat in hand, humble before the headmistress, mumbling his thanks in a half-apologetic way. Mother Gonzaga was impressed. May Tully put on a wonderful show of heartbreak. She snivelled in the corner and was sent out to get a drink of water to calm herself.

Now that Vicky's father had come to claim her and take her to a new, more promising life, I wondered what her new obsession would be. I didn't have to wait long to find out.

In front of Uncle Hermy she was uneasy. She held back, retreating into the shell she had shed soon after her arrival. She was a foreigner once more.

When Vicky came to us first she was tall for her age, and thin. All arms and legs and gawky. Not only had she filled out but she was blossoming into a lovely girl with a creamy complexion and silky raven hair. With the arrival of her father she went quiet. She became less outgoing and more withdrawn. Even Gran noticed.

'How do you feel about going to Canada?' We were in the privacy of our bedroom.

Her voice was controlled.

'He'll change his mind.' She shrugged but her manner was disturbingly reminiscent of her resentment on her arrival.

I stumbled on the object of her new obsession one day quite by accident. I was on my way home from the hairdresser late in the afternoon. It was a beautiful day. The long grass was dotted with the wild scarlet poppies of summer, and buttercups hinted yellow among the green. I bent to pick a bunch and accidentally came across Vicky and Pete sprawled in the long grass, arms entwined. He was tickling her and she snorted with laughter. I moved away, my face burning. Suddenly my young body was full of strange urges for which there was no outlet, jealousy being not the least of them. I was furious with Vicky.

'Oh sod off,' she said when I confronted her. 'You haven't a divine right to him.'

Of course she was right. Just because I was in love with him and thought that he loved me in return gave me no special claim to him. But watching her with him, the way she had to stop herself from laughing when their eyes met, the glint of pure unconcealed joy when she saw him approach, made me furious and miserable. I was a martyr, and a secret one at that. Each night I cried into my pillow, luxuriating in my great despair. First she had stolen May Tully. Now Pete Scanlon.

There was no doubt that sex was playing a major part in Vicky's physical development. Her curiosity knew no bounds, although she wasn't prepared to 'experiment', as May called it. The emotional side was a more delicate matter and I suspected that Vicky couldn't handle it.

The next afternoon I was sitting on our front steps when Pete walked past.

'Why do you prefer Vicky?' I challenged him, the hurt inside killing any pride I had.

''Cause she's different,' came the inadequate reply.

I blushed. Something about her ancestry fascinated him, I supposed. Made her more interesting in his eyes. He looked at me patronisingly in a way that set my teeth on edge and then removed himself from the gate without another word. He obviously didn't feel he owed me an explanation.

I found myself trailing after Vicky and Pete. She didn't want anyone to suspect she was seeing him so she dragged me with her everywhere, condescendingly letting me in on her little secrets as a sort of compensation. They sat side by side on the railings at the seafront, watching a fiery sun make its westward descent. They listened to the brass band on Sunday afternoons, while I moped around the bandstand or watched them mooning over one another in a sickening way, pretending I didn't exist.

'Vicky's obsession is foolish,' Gran said when she saw how easily Vicky flushed when Pete rang the doorbell.

I was glad she'd found out and did nothing to defend her. I knew Vicky was miserable at the thought of leaving Pete. She tried unsuccessfully to hide her true feelings for him under her quiet new air. I tried to hide the fact that I was delighted she was going so I would have him all to myself.

Gradually our secrets brought us closer in a strange way. Also the fact that her days with us were numbered. Uncle Hermy was waiting for the tickets to take Vicky on a steamer boat from somewhere, but he went from day to day without involving us in his plans, which annoyed Gran intensely. Getting the tickets was proving more difficult than he'd thought.

His halo was slipping because with each passing day Gran was becoming doubtful about his intentions. Was he too hiding while he cogitated on the war? She voiced her opinion aloud one day while Uncle Hermy was engrossed in the paper.

'You're a war dodger,' she told him out straight. 'Or else something's gone wrong in Canada.'

He laughed, returning his eyes to his paper.

'What a woman you are. What a woman,' he shook his head as if bowled over by her sense of humour.

He was the only person in the world who treated Gran like a joke. I couldn't help admiring him because no matter what she said he consistently refused to let her get under his skin. The truth was he didn't really care what she thought, which made him impervious to her little idiosyncrasies. This infuriated her. She stood with her lips pursed, struggling to hold her tongue in check.

'They're setting up a vigilante group,' Dad announced.

'Why?' Mam was surprised.

'People are suspicious. It's rumoured there are spies in the locality.'

'Sure, there's no spies in this country. We're neutral.'

'Hm,' Gran muttered. 'They could be here just as well as anywhere else. There are all sorts of foreigners around.' She cast Uncle Hermy a suspicious look.

Uncle Hermy couldn't be a spy, could he? He was secretive, spending long stretches in his room, reading endlessly, waiting around. When he went out he never mentioned where he was going.

'I have an appointment,' he would say and disappear.

'Who could he be visiting? He doesn't know anyone in Dublin.'

'Oh yes he does. He knows everyone, everywhere. He's been around.' Gran was resolute in her opinion.

She didn't trust him ever and now had a good excuse to keep an eye on him.

'Come on, Lizzie, we've work to do.' She hauled me up to his room to help her clean it one day when he was out.

Apart from a pair of binoculars, a compass and a small, locked suitcase, there were only his clothes and a few toiletries.

'Why is that suitcase locked?' She tried unsuccessfully to open it. 'There's a wireless set in it for sending Morse code messages to the enemy.'

'Gran!'

'Don't "Gran" me. You'll see I'm right. Somebody is getting information to the Germans. Bet it's him. Never trusted him from the minute I first laid eyes on him.'

She left the room determined to open that suitcase somehow.

Her face was mulishly stubborn as she confronted Mam.

'I'm off to Dun Laoghaire, Gertie, on an errand.' She donned her coat and hat.

'What, at this time of day?' Mam glanced at the clock.

'Don't fret, I won't be long. I've to see someone.' She retreated, mumbling to herself.

When four o'clock came and there was no sign of Gran, Mam became anxious.

'Maybe she met someone,' Vicky said.

'Maybe she did. I shouldn't have let her off on her own, but it's so long since she touched a drop of anything that I trusted her.'

Dad came home and got very agitated when Gran still hadn't shown up by teatime.

'I'm going to look for her.' He put on his hat and left.

About an hour later there was a loud knock on the front door. Mam ran up from the kitchen to open it. A young, red-faced guard stood there supporting Gran.

'Do I have the right address?' he asked.

'Of course I live here,' Gran snapped, pushing past him and weaving into the hall, the pheasant feather on her hat lacklustre and drooping.

'She waylaid me in Dun Laoghaire and demanded that your house be searched.' He was most apologetic. 'Says you're harbouring a spy against your will.'

'And a criminal,' Gran supplied.

'Nonsense.' Mam was visibly keeping herself in control. 'My husband's brother-in-law is here on holiday. That's the only visitor we have.'

'You're sure there's no trouble of any kind?' The guard looked relieved.

'Quite sure, officer, and thank you for bringing my mother-in-law home.' Mam was mortified.

'No trouble.' He left quickly, refusing a cup of tea.

Once the front door was closed Mam rounded on Gran.

'How could you? We'll be disgraced, bringing the guards to the door. You drunken old hussy.'

'Only one drop passed my lips,' Gran insisted. 'I met Mrs Turner on me way down to the garda station and she asked me into the Avenue Hotel for a small one.'

Dad came home and took Gran upstairs to her room and closed the door. We were ordered downstairs to do our homework so we couldn't eavesdrop. She spent the next week in her bedroom sulking and protesting that she was no drunk.

'There's no respect for the old and infirm any more,' she said, her voice full of self-pity.

She refused to eat and returned the trays Vicky and I trudged upstairs with untouched.

'I won't rest easy until that Hermy is in jail,' she whispered to me. 'Don't say anything to Vicky. I don't want her upset any more than she is.'

We were changing fast, Vicky and I. Though we still played hopscotch and skipping, jumping in and out of the rope shouting 'In and out through the darkie bluebells', or 'Tilly on the telephone, miss a loop, you're out', we were becoming very conscious of our new bobbing boobs. Round, firm buds. Our hips began to curve slightly too. We looked in the mirror, liking our new shape. Of course Vicky was more developed than me and she paraded every new curve and swelling up and down the bedroom like a model. The flat shapeless planes were gone for ever, now replaced by peaks and valleys that as yet retained their secrets.

Vicky measured her bust each night with a measuring tape. If it increased slightly she was delighted. Then she measured her thighs and her waist. One fraction of an inch more and she'd stop eating. Her face had lost its roundness, its contours indicating that she would soon be really beautiful. I was envious of her looks, knowing I couldn't compete. At mass on Sundays I sat red-faced and guilty while the priest intoned the seven deadly sins. I realised I was well on the way to committing all of them if I were to go on envying Vicky and being jealous of her new obsession with Pete. There was another deadly sin I was contemplating in the back of my mind. Revenge. I wanted to get my own back on her for stealing Pete Scanlon. Outside the church she looked at him, not directly but coyly. He gazed back at her, hunger in his eyes. I hated her.

A few days later I met Pete walking up Patrick Street, hands deep in his pockets, his thoughts miles away.

'Hello,' I called out.

'Hello,' he crossed the road, his smile showing strong white teeth.

'Like a knickerbocker glory?' He pointed in the direction of Mac's Ice-Cream Parlour.

'You've money to burn.' I was delighted with this attention.

'My little horse romped home,' he laughed, showing me the fistful of money he had extracted from his pocket.

As we ate our multicoloured ice-creams I could think of nothing to say and he seemed to have the same difficulty. Finally he pushed his empty glass away and, resting his head on his elbow, his eyes half-closed, he asked, 'How's Vicky?' as casually as he could make his voice sound.

I watched the dust motes dance in the light before I replied as matter-of-factly as I could. 'Oh, Vicky has a new boyfriend. Johnny Dunne,' I lied. 'She's mad about him. Talks of nothing else.' My lie was expanding rapidly. 'Anyway, she's going to Canada soon with her father.'

He looked at me gravely, his blue eyes searching mine. 'I didn't know that. Come on, I'll walk you home.'

As we came to the corner of the terrace, Vicky suddenly appeared as if from nowhere. We all stood in awkward silence, then Pete took my hand lightly.

'I'm off to England again so I'll say goodbye.' His eyes were on Vicky.

'Pete, no.' Her eyes fluttered coquettishly.

I was so full of joyful revenge I didn't register the full impact of his words. When I did I tightened my grip on his hand and said breathlessly, 'Won't you write, often?' heaving my bosom up and down. He looked down at me, then turned away.

'Well, all good things come to an end. So long.'

'Just like that?' Vicky was astonished.

I hummed tunelessly all the way home, impervious to her hysterical prattle. Revenge, oh, sweet revenge.

When Pete returned to England a few days later without calling for Vicky, she went very quiet. When he failed to answer her long letters it became obvious that he'd lost interest. She felt neglected and looked miserable. He had been a rock in the shifting sands of her existence and now that rock had perished too.

One day soon after Pete left, Uncle Hermy came home brandishing the tickets for Canada.

'Got them on the black market.'

His face was alight with happiness, unlike Vicky's which was white with shock. If there was ever any doubt that she didn't want to leave, now all trace was wiped away.

Gran hadn't succeeded in opening his suitcase and didn't want him to leave until she'd had him convicted and put in jail.

'You can't travel yet, Hermy,' she told him. 'It's too dangerous. The seas are infested with U-boats.'

'I didn't know you were concerned for my welfare.' He smiled a mocking smile.

'I'm not,' she mumbled to herself. 'I wish the sea would swallow you up.' She'd moved into the pantry out of earshot.

There was a greater emotion behind Vicky's misery. She confided in me that she was afraid of the unknown. She'd been plunged into it once before and it had worked in her favour. Now she was getting older, wiser, and less sure of herself.

She lay on her bed sobbing. Thinking she was too young for the burden of such heartbreak and emotion, I tried to console her.

'You don't understand,' she sobbed. 'I hate him. That's what. I've never told anyone before. Not another living soul. But I hate him. Blimey, Lizzie, what the hell am I going to do?'

'Who do you hate?'

'Dad.' She couldn't speak through the racking tears and I climbed into bed with her feeling closer to her than ever. 'I'd rather be dead than go to Canada with him.'

I reached for her hand, telling her soothingly that I wanted her desperately to stay, forgetting all about Pete Scanlon and my revenge. I realised now just how close we had become in spite of everything.

She took down the old framed photograph of her mother, contemplating it in dazed misery.

'Mum needs me. I know she does even though she's too self-sacrificing to say so. I'm needed to help in London. They need every able-bodied person they can get.'

All the time she was trying to convince herself of what she was saying, but she didn't succeed in convincing me.

Gran gave her piercing looks but said nothing. For once she had nothing to say, although sometimes her eyebrows shot up to her hair when she saw Vicky's look of despair. I didn't dare tell Vicky's dilemma to Mam or Gran. I was bound by a secret pact and if that were broken Vicky's tenuous friendship would be withdrawn. I couldn't take that risk.

Gran was sewing when Vicky came to sit beside her.

'There's a war on, Vick.' She turned to her. 'Up to now you've been protected from it and for that you must be grateful. Couldn't you try feeling some gratitude

143

for a change, instead of moping about feeling sorry for yourself?'

Though her words were unpalatable, they were practical as usual and seemed to compose the hollow-eyed Vicky and make her think herself less unfortunate than others. Though not much.

The pride Vicky had taken in her appearance, however bizarre, stopped altogether. She stopped experimenting with cosmetics. She stopped going around with May Tully. There was no more clumping in high heels and curling her hair. She even stopped painting her legs. May Tully's potent desire to attract men didn't interest Vicky any more, to everyone's relief.

'She's not eating,' Gran said with renewed asperity.

'It'll pass. Leave her be.' Uncle Hermy hated fuss. 'When she sees life in Canada she'll be a different person. She'll love it.'

'Hm. I wonder will she ever see it?' said Gran. 'At this rate the war will be over by the time you leave.'

I wasn't so sure.

'What are you going to do?' I asked Vicky when we were alone in our room.

Her face was hidden by the drape of her hair.

'I don't know. I haven't decided.'

For some reason I felt afraid. Although I still had no inkling of the calamity that was about to befall us, I felt an uneasiness that I couldn't decipher.

As we waited for their departure Vicky became even

more distant and lonely. She removed herself from the friendship of all the gang. She stopped sharing little confidences with me as if she didn't trust me not to tell Gran.

'What's wrong with her?' Gran was losing patience. 'Pete Scanlon wasn't such a devastating experience, you know. One swallow doesn't make a summer.'

Even Gran didn't realise how much Vicky hated having to go to live with her father in Canada. She was sulky and impatient but in unguarded moments she would toss and turn and bury her face in her pillow, unsuccessfully trying to stifle the huge sobs that racked her slight frame.

Gradually, just as I began to believe that the despair was becoming intolerable and I would have to break my silence, Vicky livened up. Her eyes took on a glitter of unhealthy excitement. She was plotting something and getting a thrill out of deceiving everyone. Except me.

Now I longed for her friendship. A real friendship like the one promised before May Tully took her under her wing and distorted her vision of the world. When I suggested that we could be best friends she became brusque to the point of brittleness. When she spoke her voice was high-pitched.

'No point. I won't be here.'

'We can write. Often.'

She looked past me with an inner dissatisfaction. She was determined not to let me break down the barrier she had erected between us brick by slow painful brick since Uncle Hermy had come home with the tickets.

'Poor child, tossed from Billy to Jack, not a thought for her feelings.' Gran spoke within earshot of Uncle Hermy.

'Stop fussing, Ma,' Dad cautioned.

'I'm not fussing. I speak as I find.' Gran sniffed. 'Poor little devil, craving for someone to love her.'

Uncle Hermy was reading about the progress of the war and was oblivious to his surroundings. Nothing Gran said, however caustic, penetrated his genial mind.

'She was so lovely. Tall and straight. Now look at her, restless and excitable.'

'Don't worry, Gran. It's her age.' Mam was more interested in John and his demands.

Vicky accepted Gran's cosseting with nothing more than her usual grimace of dissatisfaction.

'You have the appetite of a bird.' Gran tempted her with morsels of chicken or sometimes apple tart or home made soup.

Vicky subsided into silence at any mention of Canada, yet when Uncle Hermy finally announced a definite date of departure she smiled a curious resigned smile and said,

'Yes, Dad. We'll go to Canada.'

All that day there was an air of remoteness about her that was almost frightening.

* * *

On the morning of their departure Vicky's bed was empty. I thought they had left early without saying goodbye to spare us the sadness of parting. But Uncle Hermy was in the kitchen, distraught.

'She's gone. Vanished,' he kept repeating, a dazed, unbelieving expression on his face.

It took a while for me to realise that Vicky had run away. Gran was standing in her worn dressing-gown, her eyes shadowed, her face thunderous.

'If you'd left well enough alone, Hermy. But no. You always meddled. Meddled in our affairs and took my innocent daughter to that foreign country.' Gran turned the full wrath of her tongue upon him.

But Uncle Hermy only replied: 'Innocent, Sissy! Innocent, you say? Ha!'

He left the kitchen to go with Dad to do something constructive about finding Vicky. Mam was crying. John joined in, bawling his lungs out in friendly participation. The house was in uproar.

She was gone. Where? She had taken everything she possessed in Gran's old brown leather suitcase. In spite of our differences I was shocked. Where had she gone? I heard no sound in the night. Never saw her pack. I missed her instantly. I worried for her safety. Did she catch a train, or a boat? I missed our quick exchanges of views, our battles, her running commentaries on every known subject. I even missed our prolonged silences. The things we did together and the things we did separately. Though her companionship was often grudgingly given, I missed it. I thought of all the times I'd wished she'd go home to London. Now she was gone I was lonely and afraid for her.

'Gone where? Where is she?' Gran was distraught with fear for her safety.

She went to the police station with Uncle Hermy and Dad, insisting that she had to contact Sissy.

Then a telegram arrived from Auntie Sissy confirming Vicky's safe arrival in London. We were all relieved, but Gran was heartbroken.

Vicky wrote to me a week later to say she'd met up with Pete Scanlon. He was now in uniform and 'different'.

He's tense and unfriendly, not as pleased as I thought he'd be to see me. He has this strange notion that I prefer Johnny Dunne. I hate Johnny Dunne. He's about to get himself killed too, just as I return to be with him. He's Private Scanlon now and his uniform suits him. Forgive me for running off but if I'd told you you'd never have let me go without telling on me. Some day, Lizzie, when you've grown up a little more, I hope you'll understand all the reasons why I had to leave.

Meanwhile don't think too badly of me and take care of Gran.

Thank you for everything.

Your ever loving cousin,

Vicky

The next letter came on the heels of the previous one.

Dear Lizzie,
Pete has been wounded in both his legs and is hospitalised. He's having several operations, one after the other. He stares at the wall whenever I visit him and accuses me of patronising him when I try to say something comforting.

He says he will never come home until he is able to walk on his own two feet. I feel desperate. I don't know what to do to help him. He says his life is ruined.

Love Vicky

I trailed John in his pram along the town, and the pier. The mailboat stood defiantly glinting in its new white paint as it waited in the sun for its next prey. Who else would it capture and steal from my little world?

The colours of the sea sparkled before my eyes then blurred as the tears fell. Pete Scanlon injured. No wonder he didn't want Vicky around. He'd rather die than be a cripple. Or dependent.

After Vicky's disappearance Gran seemed to crumple. Tears glittered in her ravaged eyes. Uncle Hermy left quietly to get Vicky without saying goodbye to Gran. He gave Mam his small locked suitcase. She put it away safely in her bedroom.

'It'll be safe there till he gets back.'

'Back?'

'Of course he'll be back some time. It's probably a change of clothes.'

Mam was a trusting woman who hated complications and, unlike Gran, she wasn't about to create any for herself. She had enough on her plate.

Vicky's running away took its toll. Gran lost her vitality and the spring in her step and finally she took to her bed. I began to get scared, wondering what I would do without her. Doctor Pearson was sent for but after a thorough examination could find nothing wrong.

'It's just old age. She's tired and needs to rest,' she said, holding out her hand for her usual seven and sixpence.

But Doctor Pearson was thorough. She sent Gran to hospital for X-rays. Nothing showed up. She returned home and stayed in bed. Her room was depressing and airless. She mentioned dying and said she wasn't afraid as most people are. Her life had been hard, she said, but she had been given the grace to surmount her problems. She'd taken Paul's disappearance very hard, always harbouring the hope that he would return to Karen some day and not leave her the way she herself had been left with her fatherless children. She'd taken her granddaughter Vicky under her wing when she arrived in Ireland as an evacuee and looked on her as her personal responsibility, trying to give her the stability her own mother had never succeeded in giving her. Vicky had repaid her by throwing it all back in her face.

Some days she was good, almost like her old self, and

others bad. Mam wrote to Aunt Sissy to send Vicky home at once.

I sat with her. The medicine made her ramble.

'You go to school, Lizzie, and what do you learn about the ways of the world? Not practical things like how to pick a husband or rear your children. What can I pass on to you to stop you making the same mistakes I made? It wasn't easy after my Jack died. He went very young. Selfish bloody lout leaving me to fend for meself with five children. Just a bit of a farm. I built it up, though. Still, he could have waited a bit longer. Dropped dead at me feet. Such a shock. I married him when I was seventeen. Me hair still in long plaits. He was cold and unfeeling, even though my father thought it a good match. I hardly knew him. I went into that farm with nothing but a table and a few chairs. Me father gave us the bed and a few hens. The egg money was mine though. I kept it hidden in the dresser. It was all I could call me own. They all turned out all right. Got good wives. I never had much to do with Tommy's wife, her being a Yank. They all have two jobs over there so they can buy two of everything. We'll go shopping when I'm better. Remember the noise of the horses' hooves and the smells? Awful. But I like shopping. Lovely bright shopping days.'

Karen came home on sick leave. Her face was joyous when she lifted John out of his chair.

'You're so big and heavy.'

She kept looking at him as if he might suddenly

disappear if she turned away. He was full of energy, his blond mop of curls bouncing as he jumped up and down on Karen's lap.

'Little Lord Fauntleroy,' she called him and hugged his sweet-smelling body to her.

'You'll squeeze him to death,' Gran protested but John only laughed and said 'Ma Ma' and 'Da Da' to her.

Her emotions concerning Paul were shaky. Since the discovery of his letters and diaries she felt more than ever that he was alive somewhere. She refused to join the War Widows Association, saying she had nothing to contribute seeing as she wasn't even sure if she was a widow.

She couldn't or wouldn't think of Paul as missing in action. She hated the expression. She talked about him constantly, listing to Dad the places she had been to and written to, drawing comfort from her frenetic search. I think Mam would have preferred it if Karen accepted that Paul would not be coming home, but Karen sat there in the sunshine, her arms locking her body in, her eyes closed. Dreaming and thinking, thinking, thinking. Or she would sit in the kitchen in the cool of the evening with only the tick-tock of the kitchen clock for company.

'Paul's not here. I'm the only one,' she'd say, looking into the distance as if his image welled up before her from the shadows and he was there beside her like a ghost.

'It's creepy,' I said to Mam, who pursed her lips.

'Well, we're always here. She knows that. We'll help her all we can.'

She read and reread his letters. She'd become friendly with his friends during her searching. There was one of Paul's friends who was particularly kind to her. Dad shuddered when he heard that.

'She's young but she won't get involved again,' Mam said. 'She's too wrapped up in Paul's memory still.'

Karen was almost mechanical. She lived her life meaninglessly, flowing along with the tide. She collected names and wrote to senators and congressmen, qualifying her actions by telling them that Paul wasn't dead, only missing. She didn't sleep at night and took sleeping pills. She went on living but didn't live. She sent copies of his letters and photographs everywhere she thought she'd get some help in finding him. Often she didn't get any reply.

'It's hard to think and it's harder not to think,' she said, holding the photograph of Paul in uniform that she'd circulated everywhere she could think of. Beads of perspiration stood out on her forehead and her eyes were tired.

'Even if he's missing for the rest of my life, I'll never think of him as not alive.'

She blamed the RAF for not doing enough to find him. She blamed the American President for lack of interest and lack of information. She had a duty to keep up her search, she said, in case they'd forget about him altogether. She would never let them forget. She'd even talked to people who'd flown the same course, in the same planes.

'She's too wrapped up in the past. She should take better care of herself. She looks bad,' Mrs Keogh said.

Mrs Keogh was back home again with her husband intact. She seemed unscathed from her dreadful ordeal but was shocked when she saw Karen. Mrs Keogh spared nobody's feelings when she spoke her mind, which she did frequently, although her opinion was rarely sought.

'Get yourself another fella, Karen. A decent Irish bloke. Don't be wastin' your young life sitting there thinking. Stay home and don't bother about England again. Brings nothing but misery to a body.'

'The war's still going on, you know. Claiming lives every day. People I know. I have to go back,' Karen insisted.

But she made no preparations for her return. Instead, she took over caring for John, who was walking now. She washed big baskets of washing and hung them on the line, calling to John, calling to me to 'keep an eye' on him. She became fiercely protective of him and wouldn't leave him. If she decided to go out and he began to cry, she'd come back to see what was wrong with him, lift him into her arms, rocking him to and fro. Then she wouldn't leave him at all. She insulated herself with her memories and her child.

Vicky was sent back just in time to sit the primary examination. Gran insisted that she be returned to the safety of our family and Ireland.

'If that lunatic Hitler keeps up the bombings there won't be a shred of England left,' she had said, rubbing her glasses vigorously.

Her delight at Vicky's return was greater than if Vicky had been her own long-lost child, miraculously returned to her. Not once did Gran chastise her for running away. She only gazed at her lovingly, alert to her every whim. It was sickening.

'I don't know why I need this bleedin' exam,' Vicky moaned. 'What do I want Irish for, I ask you? I want to be a doctor, not a diplomat nor a telephone operator.'

'It's no weight to carry. It's your native tongue,' Gran said gently, putting a plate of fresh baked scones in front of her.

'It's not. I'm English, Gran.'

'English how are ye! How could you be English when I'm your grandmother and your mother's my daughter. Talk sense, girl.'

'I was born in England,' Vicky shouted.

'Makes no difference. You're as Irish as I am and you should be proud of it.'

However much she protested Vicky still had to sit the exam.

On the first day of the school holidays, just as we were relaxing over a late breakfast, Mam dropped a bombshell into our laps.

'You're going to boarding school next term, the pair of you.' She continued making bread. She might have said 'it's a nice day' or 'go out to play'.

'What?' Vicky looked up at her.

'You heard. Boarding school.'

'You'll toe the line there,' Gran sniffed. 'No more acting the maggot with May Tully and all that crowd. Down the road in the convent they'll be wasting their time.'

'Exactly,' Mam said. 'Whereas you'll both have less distractions where you're going. No more looking after John and worrying about Karen, and chasing the boys.' She looked pointedly at me. 'And your Irish will improve too.'

Vicky left the room speechless. Later she said to me, 'This is my punishment for running away. They're making sure I don't do it again.'

'I suppose I'm being sent as your jailer? Don't talk such rubbish, Vicky.'

'Polish up your Fáinnes. You're going west,' Gran informed us.

The first inkling we had that the chosen boarding school was very far away was when Gran said that the train fare would cost almost two pounds each. The summer stretched out before us like an eternity.

'Why are we being sent away, Gran?' I asked when we were alone one evening.

'Because your mam and fad think it's the best thing for you both. The school has produced some great scholars in the past. They're not trying to get rid of you. It's a great sacrifice for them, you know. The fees and books and uniforms. Of course, Hermy will pay for Vicky. He wants her to have a good education, I'll say that for him.'

The greater part of the sacrifice was ours. After all, I was only twelve and Vicky was thirteen. Far too young to leave home in my opinion. I was secretly glad Vicky would be with me. The thought of going so far away alone didn't bear contemplation.

Boarding School

We were up early to catch the nine o'clock train. Vicky wiped the steam from the inside of the window so she could prolong the agony of the goodbyes.

Gran waved vigorously as the train pulled out of the station, and kept waving until she was only a dot in the distance. Dad stood beside her, stoical and staring, supporting her waving arm.

'I hope our trunk is safe in the luggage compartment.' I stared out the window so Vicky wouldn't see the tears starting up again.

'I hope it gets lost.' Her voice was sullen, her eyes dry.

All that sewing on of name-tapes on double everything done by Gran and Mam. All that new underwear, not to mention the new uniforms. Then there were the parcels of sweets, cakes and biscuits, presents from the staff of the Home and Colonial and our neighbours and friends. Friends and neighbours. Thinking of them brought on a new bout of weeping and Vicky said, 'Shut your trap, Lizzie Doyle. You're not a baby,' and stared stoney-faced out the window. She looked as ridiculous as I felt in her stiff grey serge uniform and stupid wide-brimmed hat centred with a crest that bore the school motto. Something in Latin that I couldn't read.

There was a taxi waiting for us at Ballygrange station to transport us to the convent. After endless miles along bumpy roads we turned into a tree-lined avenue, at the end of which stood a huge white uncompromising institute that had to be the school.

'Well, here ye are.' The taxi driver dumped the trunk unceremoniously at our feet. 'I've another load to collect.' He jumped into his taxi and was off.

A statue of the Blessed Virgin smiled down on us and we mounted the steps and rang the bell.

'Welcome to Saint Aloysius's,' said the tall nun who answered the door. 'I'm Sister Stella Maris, your headmistress.'

'I'm Vicky and this is my cousin Lizzie.' Vicky always took it upon herself to make the introductions.

The nun shook hands and smiled thinly.

'Follow me.' She led us along highly polished corridors, up bare wooden stairs to our dormitory, only the rattle of her beads and the clomping of our shoes breaking the silence.

'This is the wash-room if you'd like to wash your hands.' Her hand gestured towards the double row of wash hand-basins. 'And the dressing-room.'

We followed her into an empty room lined with

cupboards. She assigned us a cupboard each, with shelves and pigeon-holes for shoes.

'You may unpack when Joe brings up your trunk. If you'd like a cup of tea I'll take you down to the refectory.' She spoke in clipped, economical sentences.

We hung up our hats and coats and followed her through another maze of corridors and stairs. She walked as rapidly as she talked. The refectory was a long room with rows and rows of scrubbed deal tables. We were served tea and plain buns by a little nun in a checked apron.

'The others will be here before you know it.' She smiled warmly as if bestowing good news. But we dreaded meeting 'the others'.

Sister Stella Maris left us to our own devices and went to prepare herself to greet more new arrivals.

'Bloody prison,' Vicky mouthed as tears shone in her eyes. I nodded, unable to speak.

By six o'clock the refectory was full. The seniors marched about, confident and important, talking loudly about the holidays and the boys they were crazy about at present. The bell rang for tea.

'Making it all up,' Vicky sneered and turned to the girl beside her who was obviously new because she was crying. 'Stop blabbin',' she told her, not unkindly. 'Here, have my sausages. I don't eat them.'

Tea was sausages and bread and butter. Vicky ate nothing.

'You'll be hungry later. Eat up.' Sister Stella stood beside her but Vicky still wouldn't eat. The bread was coarse and grey but I was hungry enough to eat mine.

We went for a walk around the grounds in a crocodile and, after the rosary in the chapel and thanksgiving for our safe delivery to our new school, we were escorted to our dormitory. A senior was assigned to each dormitory.

Our senior stood at the end of the rows of white quilted beds, surrounded by white curtains covered in tiny specks of mould. She looked as forbidding as any nun as her eyes roamed the room. We washed in freezing water, then knelt beside our beds to say our night prayers.

'I'm not staying here,' Vicky whispered from the next bed.

'Silence,' called the senior.

'Bloody cheek,' Vicky retorted but only audible to me.

'You're not going to run away,' I whispered from my icy bed, terrified that, if she did, I'd be all alone.

'Not bleedin' likely. When I write to Mum and tell her about this set-up, she'll be over to take me out at once.'

I lay back with relief.

'Vicky Rosenblume and Lizzie Doyle, get out of your beds.'

We jumped out and pulled back the curtains, thinking that by some miracle we'd been sent for to go home.

'No talking in the dormitory.' Sister Stella stood unsmiling. 'Didn't you read the sign on the door? Next time you'll be separated. Understood?'

'Yes, Sister.' We shivered with cold and fright in our unfamiliar regulation nightdresses.

'You're together as a special concession. Kindly respect that.' She was gone, gliding away as silently as she had come.

'She's got wings in her back,' Vicky whispered.

Her feet didn't seem to touch the ground all right. Perhaps she was already a saint.

Time at the convent was measured by a different bell toll to that of the outside world.

We were roused at six-thirty to the chant of 'Praise the Lord', to which we learned to reply instantly 'And his blessed mother and all the angels and saints', in thick, sleep-filled voices.

After mass we had a breakfast of lumpy porridge and more bread and tea. School started at nine o'clock sharp. Break at eleven. Dinner was served at twelve-thirty, usually a grey messy stew and jacket potatoes. Occasionally there was cabbage or turnips from the kitchen garden. Tea at five was bread and jam again, or sausages, with an egg and fried potatoes on Fridays. The routine never varied, except on Saturdays when we played hockey or basketball and Sundays when we went for long walks. Girls who had injuries were exempted.

The tuck shop opened before the walk, so we could eat sweets and talking was permitted. Those two concessions lessened the dreary miles through the bleak countryside.

Gradually I settled into the routine. Vicky didn't.

One morning about a month after our arrival Vicky refused to eat her porridge.

'It's time to stop this nonsense,' a senior said and sent for Sister Stella Maris.

'Eat it,' she said, standing over Vicky, slowly enunciating each syllable.

Vicky sat motionless, head bent. I felt her misery like a ball in the pit of my stomach. Sister Stella Maris stood rigid, her rosary coiled around fingers bunched into a fist.

Rage burned on Vicky's face and manifested itself in two flaming spots on her cheeks. But she confronted her plate obstinately, making no attempt to eat the congealed grey mess.

The school bell rang. No one dared move.

'Your parents made no provision for a special diet for you. Therefore you have no choice but to eat what's put in front of you.'

Vicky sat, eyes defiantly on her plate.

'Making such a fuss about a few lumps in your porridge is a bad example to the other girls. If you refuse to eat the food we provide, you'll have to leave this school.'

Vicky jumped up. 'I'll go and pack,' she said triumphantly.

'Sit down.' Sister's face was red with rage.

'It's poisonous. I can't eat it,' Vicky shouted.

'The others manage. They even grow up strong and healthy. Look at the seniors.'

Vicky's eyes roamed around the refectory.

'Cows, the lot of them. Country heifers. They'd eat pig swill.'

'Vicky,' I hissed, terrified for her.

Sister Stella Maris's eyes were hot embers of rage.

'Stand up and apologise at once to the whole school for your outrageous behaviour.' Words were beginning to fail her.

Vicky scraped back her chair and mumbled, 'Sorry.'

'Louder,' shouted Sister Stella.

'I'm sorry,' Vicky shouted.

'Dismissed,' Sister Stella Maris shouted back and Vicky flounced off in a mood of revenge. The rest of us trailed out silently.

From then on Vicky went through the motions of speaking when spoken to in monosyllables. She was poker-faced and indifferent.

'That bloody bitch'll be glad to see the back of me yet,' she informed me malevolently. 'She'll pay me to leave. Mark my words.'

Her schoolwork was suffering and she blamed the 'rotten nuns' who taught us on her constant failure to keep up with the rest of the class. She was permanently furious and only spoke to the rest of the class in low spiteful murmurs, inciting rage among us all.

'I'll never be able to do medicine now. There isn't even a bleedin' science teacher here in this neck of the woods.'

I couldn't help feeling sorry for her, even though I found her behaviour embarrassing. She was used to being the best in class in the National school. Now she seemed to have undergone a complete change.

One Saturday after dinner and just before Games we were brassing our inkwells and Vicky's face was a study in despair.

'I've got to have a fag. Come on, Lizzie. Keep nicks for me.'

We sneaked out the side door past Sister Assumpta who was on duty and almost blind.

I followed Vicky downstairs along the nuns' corridor, which was out of bounds, into the garden and up to the graveyard, where she scaled the wall expertly while I kept watch. I picked shallots for Vicky so her breath wouldn't give her away.

She returned shortly and we ran to the shed behind the playing fields and she sat smoking and coughing alternately.

'I hate this bloody place.' Vicky was practising the art of blowing perfect smoke rings. I watched them disperse into the cold air.

'It's not that bad. You'll get used to it.'

'Never,' she vowed. 'You're letting yourself get brainwashed by those bitches.'

'Quick, someone's coming.' We raced round the back of the playing fields, Vicky stuffing the loose cigarettes down the front of her gymslip.

But she was caught and hauled into Sister Stella Maris's office where she was given a good talking to. Some civic-minded soul had felt duty bound to report that a junior was buying cigarettes in a shop in the town.

The nuns' tolerance of Vicky's melodramatic outbursts was amazing. Auntie Sissy wrote and advised her to settle down and work. That was a great blow to her pride. Gran sent a postal order for two pounds in a brown envelope with a cautionary word for Vicky: 'Be a good girl and make your old gran proud.'

'She's as bad as the rest.' Vicky's lip trembled and she bit it to fight back the tears but her behaviour didn't improve. She was often sent to the chapel to recite three rosaries with poor old Sister Ambrose, who prayed very slowly and whistled through her teeth, or chewed them while she prayed.

She picked on the old defenceless nuns, or the postulants, like she picked wings off flies, or stems off daisies. When she got into trouble she blamed her absent parents, her prison-like surroundings. Anything or anyone but herself. She hated the place with a violence she usually reserved for loved ones. Vicky truly believed that no one loved or cared about her.

Until one Wednesday afternoon when we were walking in the grounds during break-time. A taxi drove up to the convent door and Gran hauled herself out, complaining about the low, uncomfortable seats. All eyes turned to stare.

'Gran,' Vicky shrieked, running and throwing herself at Gran before she had time to straighten herself up and adjust her hat.

The whole school watched in amazement as Gran paid the taxi driver while we lifted out bags and parcels of shopping.

'You haven't come for good?' Vicky lifted and hauled the bags up to the hall door theatrically.

I wondered if through sheer spite and deviousness she had engineered this whole operation. She loved drama and had the vitality to keep it alive while wearing out the nuns and everybody around her. She knew Gran couldn't tell the difference between her false emotions and her real ones any more. She played on her sympathy.

'Vicky,' Gran admonished as soon as she was settled in the best parlour. 'You've worked us all up into a fine state. What happened to my bright, confident granddaughter who never gave a minute's trouble in her life?'

She had conveniently forgotten the trouble Vicky had caused when she ran away.

Vicky hung her head and sighed and said, 'Oh, Gran, you've no idea how awful it is here.'

'We'll soon find out,' Gran assured her.

We left while Gran was revived with a nice tea then we were sent for officially. This time Reverend Mother and Sister Stella Maris were present. They were seated around a highly polished table. Reverend Mother beckoned us to sit down. Then Gran launched forth at the nuns, directing her pitch at Reverend Mother.

'Vicky's a nice ordinary girl who needs encouragement. But because she's clever she's sensitive and needs careful handling.'

'She's a troublemaker,' Reverend Mother stated without raising her voice. 'She must learn to abide by the rules of the school or it'll be a great disadvantage to her in later years.'

'She wants to do medicine.' Gran came straight to the point. 'She tells me there's no science teacher.'

'No,' Sister Stella Maris conceded, her colour rising. 'But Vicky doesn't even go to the trouble of learning what's on the syllabus.'

Vicky played her part by drooping and sighing.

'Nothing is ever what it seems.' Gran spoke sharply to Sister Stella Maris. 'The child is hungry. You can't learn on an empty stomach. That's why I've brought all this food,' she leaned over to draw attention to the loaves of bread and pots of jam among the goodies. Reverend Mother leaned with her and nearly had a seizure.

'We don't allow bread in food parcels. There's plenty provided.'

'What use is it if they can't eat it? She comes from a good home.'

Vicky and I slid down our seats in semi-obscurity.

'Now,' Gran continued to the speechless nuns, 'here's what you'll do. Get her a science teacher.'

'There isn't . . .'

'Scour the country. Find one. Her father will pay.'

Vicky looked up in amazement but Gran's face was set.

'Vicky wants to succeed. Don't you?'

Vicky nodded.

'I'll go to the shops in the morning and leave an order to be delivered to the girls at regular intervals, seeing as they don't have any visitors. After all, Reverend Mother, you don't want these precious children in your care growing up ignorant just for the want of a bit of decent food.'

She stood up, smoothed the wrinkles out of her best tweed coat, adjusted the plumes over her right ear and said, 'Now if you'll excuse me I have to have a little rest. If you'll be kind enough to phone the hotel to book me a room for the night,' she looked at Reverend Mother.

'There isn't a hotel in the town, Mrs Doyle.' Her voice shook.

'Then I'll have to stay here.' Gran sat down again and beamed. ''Twas a long oul' journey.'

Reverend Mother left to arrange for one of the nun's cells to be prepared for Gran's overnight stay, with Sister Stella Maris close on her heels.

'Oh Gran. I lie awake and think of us all separated. Lizzie and me here among strangers. You and Auntie

Gertie lonely for us.' She began to cry and I joined in.

'Stuff and nonsense,' said Gran. 'We're all hail and hearty. All you've got to do is learn your lessons and get on.'

'But you don't understand. In this jail I'm not a complete person.'

'Cut the cackle. You'll shape up fine. Look at Lizzie there bearing up. Aren't you Lizzie, love?'

'Yes, Gran. I don't mind so much.'

One of the lay nuns returned to take Gran off and we went back to school.

'Traitor,' Vicky rounded on me when we were out of earshot.

'You're just a selfish pig,' I retorted. 'Dragging Gran all the way here. And at her age too. Just to add another bit of drama to your useless life.'

'I was longing to see her . . .'

'So you wrote all your complaints and miseries to her, not stopping to think that the long journey could have killed her.'

'How was I to know she'd come?'

'What did you think? You always had her wrapped around your little finger.'

'I hate you!' She ran off, slamming a door somewhere, rocking the foundations of the convent.

'She's very unhappy.' Gran looked concerned as we walked slowly down the avenue next morning.

'She doesn't care who she tramples on to get her own way.' I was tired of sticking up for Vicky.

'You should pull together. After all, you, Lizzie, have good, solid parents. Vicky has . . .' She stopped, her lips compressed. 'There's only the two of you.' Her eyes misted over.

'But Vicky likes being unhappy and drawing attention to herself,' I insisted.

'She doesn't really. Now what's keeping her? I could do with a cup of tea. You'd like a nice scone or a cream bun, wouldn't you?'

From then on Vicky suffered school with the air of a sad elephant confined to a small space, when one or other of the twenty nuns was around. But behind their backs she was still theatrical, overstating everything, and emphasising her emotions with extravagant gestures. Gradually she became popular because she spent so much time tempting our classmates into orgies of deceit. All meaningless frivolity. But she studied hard. By the end of the school term she'd settled down in spite of herself.

Gran's delight at having her lost grandchildren returned to the bosom of the family for the Christmas holidays couldn't have been greater.

'This is the best Christmas present of all,' she announced, handing us our reports.

Mine was average. Vicky had got an A in Science and Maths and Bs in every other subject. Her future was sealed.

'It'll be Doctor Vicky next,' said Gran.

'Did Dad mind paying extra for the Science teacher?' Vicky asked.

'I never enquired. Just sent him the bills.'

'You know Hermy wants Vicky to get a good education,' said Dad who was intent on carving the turkey.

'Yes. That's true. When he sees your Fáinne, Vicky, he'll be so proud.'

We went through five boring years of routine, each holiday drawing us further apart from the now splintered 'gang'. John grew up rapidly behind our backs. We felt cheated of his babyhood. Suddenly we saw Dun Laoghaire differently. There was so much more to notice. To savour.

Like the ice-cream parlour, where they served homemade creamy cones for a penny. The chip shop, where a twopenny bag of golden chips, served in newspaper, warmed our hearts. We spent the holidays getting messages for Mam and any other mother who needed them. Food was our obsession. We bought fresh buttered eggs from the Monument Creamery and salty yellow country butter. We ate bread and mixed fruit jam in May Tully's or bread and sugar.

'Only the lowest of the low buy mixed fruit jam.' Gran was horrified.

We didn't care. Nothing tasted nicer than bread and jam in someone else's house. Even May Tully's. Woolworth's was a treasure trove. We had a choice of two cinemas. The tennis club in Sandycove. The baths for swimming in the summer or the open sea. The rocks to climb or fish for crabs or tiddlers with jam jars tied with string and butterfly nets.

We acted like strangers at home, speaking when spoken to and never really relaxed with our family as before.

'We've become institutionalised,' said Vicky sadly.

But it did us good. The terms and the years flew by and we passed all our exams with flying colours.

Uncle Hermy came over specially for our 'Graduation Ceremony', and sat proud as punch beside Gran. She managed to be pleasant enough to him until he announced that he was definitely taking Vicky back to Canada with him to study medicine there. And Vicky wanted to go.

'It's a good opportunity for Vicky,' said Dad.

'She's his daughter,' said Mam.

'Bad cess to him,' said Gran.

'I can't wait,' said Vicky.

'I'll miss you, Vicky,' I told her. And this time I really meant it.

We were like sisters.

Pete Scanlon

It snowed. High and deep. White snow everywhere; on my new boots as I stamped my feet on the steps, sending fine flurries flying in all directions. It caught on the trees and the window ledges and built up on the parapet and chimneys. Solid, quieting the world, turning it whiter. It snowed night and day. The snow plough rumbled through the main streets scattering trailing sand in its wake. The children plunged into it 'gathering up the crystal mantle to freeze'.

'Look at the trees,' they cried. 'Look at the trees.'

I trudged home throwing snowballs with freezing hands covered in wet knitted mittens. The kitchen was warm and brighter than I'd ever remembered. Mam stood at the table peeling potatoes. She was thinner and seemed hunched as she leaned over her task.

The fire burned brightly, reflecting its orangey warmth on to the twilight snow outside, making it yellow and luminous as the sky darkened. An eerie quietness prevailed. Gran's cartwheels of soda bread sat on the cooling rack, and the kitchen was full of cooking smells and airing clothes.

'It's like the grave without John,' Mam said, echoing my thoughts.

'They'll be home before you know it.'

'I wonder. She's very taken with North Carolina and the timber ranch. If you ask me she's very taken with Paul's cousin Hank. My God, what a name. It's enough to make a body nervous.'

'It's just that he's been so kind to them and the interest he takes in John.'

'I suppose it's natural enough,' Mam sighed. 'It's all they've left of Paul. But I can't help wondering . . .'

She sighed again and put the potatoes on to boil, afraid to voice her fear that Karen might fall for Paul's cousin in case it would come true.

But Karen would never fall in love with Paul's cousin, would she? Or take John so far away from his adoring family? What was best for John would be her main concern. And surely that would be to keep him in a stable environment now that he was attending the National school. He marched off with Karen every morning, a sturdy little boy with cropped wavy hair and a big schoolbag full of treats.

'It's this weather, Gertie. I've never seen so much snow in my life. It makes you feel sort of cut off from the rest of the world.' Gran sat with her skirts lifted to the flames. 'Sit down here, Lizzie. It's enough to freeze a body out there.'

Dad too missed Karen and John. He went about his daily life cheerfully enough, yet he still expected to be surprised by that little tornado jumping out at him any minute. Most of all we missed John's constant stream of chatter. I picked up his pearl-handled gun, thrown carelessly aside, and tried to picture him in America.

He grew up so fast while we were at boarding school. Gran bemoaned the loss of his corkscrew curls that Mam had insisted on cutting. Vicky and I missed the little baby he once was.

The snow swirled in large flakes, the whining wind sweeping it up in drifts along the ground. I lay awake wondering about Karen and John and their future.

Paul's parents had sent the tickets for the holiday. They were anxious to see their only grandchild and felt that, now he was six, he was old enough to travel. Karen had jumped at the opportunity to meet Paul's parents. It rekindled her burning ambition to find him and talk about him. She had been living in a kind of inertia for so long that the trip could only do her good.

She had gone to London for the Victory celebrations, hoping that if prisoners were released she'd be there to welcome Paul home. Victory flags hung everywhere. Windows stayed open after dark, light shining boldly from them. London was coming to life after the strain of nearly six years of war. But when the end eventually came there was no huge explosion of excitement. It crept up on them with snippets of information and announcements. First the collapse of Germany, then Mussolini's murder and the liberation of all the capital cities. Finally, on the evening of 7 May 1945 it was announced that the war in Europe was won.

The war years had made people reckless; perhaps it was the uncertainty of the future or the unreality of the circumstances. Karen had been an unwitting casualty. She went to St Paul's for the Victory service on a glorious day with a bank holiday atmosphere and then to Whitehall where crowds surged around the Air Ministry to watch Winston Churchill appear on the balcony. He said to the hushed crowd, 'This is your victory.' And they cheered and cheered and she cried for Paul as their cheers carried through the heart of London.

Then the GIs left, draining the city. Huge convoys of army vehicles rolled away, leaving a shattered London to pick itself up. No more chewing-gum and nylons, candy and chocolate bars in abundance. No more Paul.

She left London to the strains of Vera Lynn singing 'We'll Meet Again', realising for the first time that she and Paul would never meet again.

On a dull blowy day in early March we stood in a little group watching the mailboat glide into the harbour bringing home Private Peter Scanlon, who had finally been invalided out of the army and was now a hero in the eyes of his family and friends. His mother had organised a welcome party and had included me in her list of invitations to celebrate Pete's homecoming. I was surprised and flattered, shy and excited, all at once.

Finally he came down the gangplank, neat and spruce in civvies, and smiled in surprise when he saw us all. But the smile didn't reach his eyes. He was tired and walked stiffly with the aid of a walking stick, with a tension in him that he held in tight control. It spoke of the intolerable times he had lived through. Times that had obviously stretched him mentally as well as physically to the limit.

The carefree, mischievous Pete Scanlon whom I hadn't seen for years had changed. I felt ill-at-ease and gauche, not knowing what to say, yet feeling the tension rise in the back of my neck and spread down my spine.

I was tired too, I realised. The whole world was probably tired. The war was over and there was a sort of anti-climax. The world's wounds were not yet healed. Deprivation and shortages were everywhere. Ireland continued on much the same, in a state of low-grade poverty, hopelessly living from hand to mouth.

Cold, stiff and uncomfortable, Pete nonetheless graciously accepted our welcome and our congratulations. He would have a disability pension from the British Government for the rest of his life, his mother boasted. A life that would have to be rebuilt. I didn't wait for the party she'd planned because I felt too awkward, so I left on a pretext.

I called in to see him a few days later. In the faint hall light his face was in shadow but he smiled and brought me into the kitchen, where his mother put the kettle on. The silence seemed to gather and grow, as Jimmy Scanlon sat at the table giving a good imitation of industrious eating, head bent, eyes on his plate, ears alert.

In the dim light of the kitchen Mrs Scanlon's hair looked dishevelled, her clothes crumpled. She seemed to feel the awkwardness of my presence that even the pouring out of the tea did not dispel. The adjustments to her son's new status as a 'hero' were taking their toll. Gone was her buoyant laughing Pete. He sat looking at me with luminous sad eyes.

'How are you keeping, Lizzie?' His expression was grave but his eyes were alight with interest.

'I'm fine, thanks.'

'You look great.'

I was liberally painted with powder and rouge, to cover my pale face and the deep shadows beneath my eyes more than to impress him.

Pete chain-smoked as he drank his tea and we talked in generalities about old school friends and neighbours. Any mention of the war was studiously avoided. So was any mention of Vicky.

'Now that you've left school, what are you going to do?' he asked as though he really wanted to know.

'Nursing.'

'So you'll be off over to England?'

'No. Mam and Dad won't hear of me going to England. They're willing to let me train in St. Michael's though.'

'Hm. Can't say I blame them. Poor Karen didn't fare so well there,' said his mother.

'What put nursing into your head?' Pete asked.

'I've always wanted to be a nurse. Can't remember a time when I didn't.'

'So it's no surprise to anyone then?'

'No. What about you? What are your plans?'

He stood up, hands deep in his pockets, and turned stiffly towards the window.

'I can't wait to be operational again. I'm just stagnating here.'

'Hear hear,' said Jimmy with a grin. Finding the conversation uninteresting he picked up his jacket and left.

'Nonsense,' his mother protested from the hall as she prepared to return to work.

'You mean you're going back into the army?' I had difficulty keeping my voice steady.

'No. That's just technical jargon. What I mean is I want something to do. I can't mope around here for ever, getting in the way.'

'But you're only just home. Give yourself a chance. After all, your injuries were pretty severe from what I gather.'

His face was impassive.

'I'm fine now as you can see,' he shrugged. 'In another

few months when I've built up my strength I'll be completely recovered.'

'That's marvellous, Pete, isn't it?'

He dismissed my delight with an embarrassed shrug.

'Is it?' He smiled humourlessly. 'I think you were right that time you tried to persuade me to stay on at school. I'm a bit short on qualifications now. Not even a trade under my belt.'

'You have your army training. That must count for something. And a disability pension for the rest of your life. Guaranteed pay if you don't work another day.'

Pete extinguished his cigarette during the awkward silence that followed.

'Who wants a disability pension!' He looked disgusted.

'What do you think you'd like to do?'

I knew as well as he did that his choices were limited, I also knew that jobs were scarcer than ever.

He shrugged again. 'I liked the army. I liked the action. I got a thrill out of the danger. Don't get me wrong, I was just as scared as the next fella, but it was challenging, exciting. Survival was the name of the game and you played that game for all your worth or you didn't live to tell the tale. I loved the risks we took. I loved being one of a powerful group who held the balance of life and death. It's hard for you to imagine, I'm sure, but I hated it when I had to sign out.'

He spoke with passion. Watching his animated face and the reflection of the fire dance in his eyes as he gazed into it, it wasn't difficult to believe him. Then he turned to look at me, his expression challenging, defying me to tell him he was wrong to have felt like that. I didn't say anything, just returned his gaze. The animation left him just as suddenly and his eyes were flat and dead. I'd been given a glimpse of his inner feelings.

'I'm no hero, Lizzie. My motives weren't even honourable. I wanted action and that's what I got. This,' he pointed to his gammy leg, 'is the legacy.'

Then he laughed at his own pun and the awkwardness shifted.

'It was either kill or be killed.' He had that shuttered expression on his face again.

Then the old mocking smile returned.

'War is a game and playing games was always what I liked to do best, as you know. Now the time has come for me to grow up.'

He leaned against the jamb of the door to say goodbye as I left.

'You mustn't blame yourself for the fact that you got injured. It just happened. The price for all the excitement you had.'

He laughed.

'Don't let bad experiences cloud your belief in yourself.'

'You should be a philosopher, not a nurse.'

He moved closer, scrutinising my face, making me blush as a tremor of excitement shot through me.

'I must go. I'll see you again.' I made for the gate as fast as I could.

When I did see him again he greeted me with a veneer of good humour, but underneath he was in bad form.

Mam said his mother was worried about him.

'It's a natural reaction to what he's been through,' Dad said. 'The world went mad over there and he lived through it all.'

'He said he enjoyed the experience, Dad.'

'Perhaps at the time he thought he did. He's paying for it now. He's probably shell-shocked.'

We'd all heard of shell-shock and how the asylums were full of poor creatures who'd suddenly and unexpectedly lost their nerve and gone mad.

'Pete is just a bit disoriented. He needs to be rehabilitated.'

Jimmy called a few days later.

'He wants to know if you'd like to go to the flicks?'

Jimmy was tall and gangly for his age. He was working in the coalyard in Dun Laoghaire helping to unload some of the shipment of American coal that Ireland had just taken delivery of. It was temporary work but Jimmy was glad of the money. He thought he was the bee's knees because he had a few shillings to rattle in his pocket, which he did continually while he spoke.

'Why doesn't he ask me himself?'

'He doesn't go out much. Ma says it'd do him good to

get out. There's a great one on in the Pavilion. Bing Crosby and Fred Astaire in *Blue Skies*.'

That's how we came to be sitting in the dimness of the Pavilion cinema with his arm stretched casually along the back of my seat. Close together we sat absorbed while Bing sang 'Blue skies, nothin' but blue skies'. Tears stung as my own sadness mingled with the cheerful happy words of the song. I thought about Karen so far away with John in America, and Mam so reluctant to let him go. But when the invitation had arrived, Karen was adamant. Now our house was like a morgue without them.

Pete leaned towards me and gently brushed away a tear.

'It's only a film.' He moved closer and took my hand in his.

When he kissed me a rush of excitement coursed through me. Quickly he released me and we moved back from one another, neither one of us knowing who was the more surprised.

We walked home slowly and silently, content in each other's company. The night air was chilly. Pete walked painfully up the hill. I linked him casually hoping he wouldn't think I was helping him along. When we reached our house I opened the gate, but Pete made no attempt to follow me.

'Maybe we could do this again some time?' he said.

'I'd love that.'

'You'd better go in. That coat isn't the warmest.'

'I beg your pardon! It mightn't look it but this coat is pure wool. Cost me four pounds and twenty coupons.'

I did a twirl.

'Well for the idle rich!'

'It was a birthday present.'

'Do you remember that fur coat of yours? Whatever happened to it?'

'Gran made a rug to put in front of the fire out of it. Didn't like to see it perishing away on the hall stand.'

Pete's laughter rang out.

'We had some good times. All the gang are scattered now.' He looked away.

'Yes.'

'Best say goodnight then.'

He took my hands in his, pulling me to him. He kissed me gently as if he were afraid I might break. Then he pulled me closer and kissed me again. Suddenly and fiercely this time, holding me as if he would never let me go. Just as suddenly he released me, said goodnight and was gone, slowly retracing his steps home, the tap–tap of his walking stick sounding lonely and vulnerable in the dark.

I stood touching my lips, remembering his kiss for a long time after the light clicked on in his bedroom down the road and the swish of the old faded curtains blocked it out again. The night was perfectly still, the stars brilliant in the frosty sky.

'Come in, you'll catch your death,' Gran called from the hall door, and waited until I ran lightly up the steps. I had never dreamed that I could want anything as much as I had wanted that kiss. I ran past her up the stairs, my hands covering my face to hide my burning cheeks. But she followed me into my bedroom.

'Late to be coming in.' She sat herself down on the edge of the bed.

'It's only after eleven.' I glanced at my watch.

'He's a nice enough boy, I suppose?' Gran had her eyes fixed on my reflection in the mirror.

'He's lovely, Gran.'

'Mind you, don't get too fond of him. You're too young for any commitment and, besides, didn't Vicky get herself into an awful muddle over him?'

'That wasn't his fault.' I turned to face her.

'He encouraged her enough at the time. 'Twas only when she followed him to England that he cooled off. Men are all the same. They have to be doing the chasing or else they're not interested.'

'I'll remember that, Gran.' I bent to kiss her good night.

'By the way, Lizzie, will you put a shilling each way on Black Beauty for me tomorrow? It's too cold for me to go out.' She handed me two shillings wrapped in a bit of paper with 'Black Beauty' written on it.

'You still like a little flutter,' I laughed.

'Very occasionally. Only when one of me favourites is

winning. I see your Pete Scanlon in the bookies sometimes. Fond of a little flutter himself. Now I'm off to finish me rosary. God bless.'

She was gone off to her room, her mind firmly fixed on the Lord, now that her bet was as good as placed.

I wrote to Vicky in Canada telling her all the news, secretly glad she wasn't around at present.

Vicky

V icky and I kept in touch, writing to one another
quite regularly.

Dear Lizzie,
I can't tell you what a shock it was to discover Aunt Hilda's
house was so dark and stale. At first glance it was more like a
museum, with overstuffed sofas and a collection of ancient
photographs and mementos from the 'old country'. It made me
want to throw up.

I'm getting used to it now but I had expected Canada
to be new and shining white and modern. How wrong can you
be!

The older women wear black all the time. They are
mostly fat and talk about the 'old country' incessantly because
that's where they're from. Aunt Hilda is Daddy's aunt so,
as you can imagine, she's older than God. It's so cold here that
I frost over while waiting for the bus to college and I'm
crying with the cold by the time I get there. Well the tears are
there.

Of course I'm only here for a while until I finish college and then I'll be going home. I'm not sure if that's to London or to you. You never know your luck! You might find me standing on the doorstep one day soon.

College isn't bad except for the sports. You know I always hated hockey. But I enjoy cutting up frogs. The girls are big and strong and play ice hockey. The cold doesn't seem to bother them at all. I can't play but I won't get away with that excuse for much longer. Dad is paying for coaching for me. He's just waiting to find the best coach.

My best friend is Jewish. She is the tallest, strongest girl in the class. She brought me home last week. Her house sits on the top of a hill with nothing but fields for miles around it. Her father's fields. She has a brother who's dark and handsome and sexy looking. I hope she'll invite me back soon because her mother seems to cook all day long.

Now when I go back tonight I'll have to weigh myself. Of course if I take up this damn hockey my thighs will expand and become huge and muscly like the other girls'. Oh despair, I don't seem to have much choice.

Love to your mam and dad, and of course to Gran.

Your loving cousin,

Vicky

Dear Lizzie,

Horror of horrors, my mother has arrived and I wish with all my heart she'd stayed in her beloved London. She embarrasses me with her wailing and moaning in front of Daddy's relations.

She's for ever recounting her deeds of heroism to anyone who will listen and her acts of bravery are taking on magnum proportions with each telling. I'm dead ashamed. She sits exchanging hardship stories from morning till night. Why Daddy insisted on her joining us I don't know. It isn't as if they even get on well together. The long separation hasn't mended anything between them. Another disaster the war has left in its wake. They're like strangers, with him buried in the newspaper while she wails that she wants to go home and accuses him of depriving her of helping to build up London again now that they've won the war. It must be hard on her all the same after all she did during the terrible times to be deprived of living there now in relative comfort. He says he's obliged to keep our little family intact. I wish he wouldn't make such sacrifices for my sake. Mum cries a lot and gets flustered in her homesickness for her friends and her beloved London. Daddy works all the time making money to send me to a posh college.

One thing though. There are no shortages here. The fruit is plentiful and delicious. I've given up the aniseed balls – too fattening! I'm on a very strict diet which is difficult to keep to with such choices to eat.

I'm glad you met up with Pete Scanlon again and that he's home safely. Give him my regards. I hope he gets fixed up in a suitable job. He could always take up singing.

I've decided I prefer the tall, dark, handsome types like my new friend Emily's brother, David. I'll send on a photograph if I can get one.

Write to me all about Karen and John. I miss Gran. Tell her
I think of her often, especially when I get lonely for Ireland.
  Love to all,
  Your ever loving cousin,
  Vicky

I wrote to Vicky by return, giving her all the news, omitting any details about Pete Scanlon.

I didn't see Pete but I heard from Jimmy that he had got an apprenticeship with Huet Motors. Jimmy told me he went to work every day on the bus and found it tiring.

'He loves the cars. Loves messin' with engines. I wouldn't be surprised if he buys himself an old banger and does it up,' Jimmy informed me.

'That'd be great. He could take your mother out for a drive in the country sometimes.'

'Hm.'

'How's he keeping otherwise?'

'Grand.'

I had a nagging feeling in the back of my mind that Pete was avoiding me.

I went to the local tennis club hop with Pauline and Tess. Pete was lounging in a corner with a group of lads, his walking stick propped against the wall beside him.

'Hi,' I called over to him, but he returned my greeting with only the faintest of smiles and a bare nod of recognition before returning his attention to the engrossing discussion he was involved in before I interrupted him.

He didn't ask me to dance. He didn't dance with anyone else either. Maybe he felt awkward about dancing. I kept out of his way, stung by his studious avoidance, and walked home with the girls.

The summer holidays stretched ahead once more. Long hot days to do what we liked with before we each went our separate ways again in September. May Tully was working in Liptons. She had left school just before her Intermediate exam, her longing to make money outweighing her need of further education.

She was tall and slender now, neat in her snow-white shop coat. She was an aspiring actress, a member of the local amateur dramatic society. She was supposed to be engaged to the leading man in the cast of their latest production.

'Well if it isn't little Lizzie Doyle,' she greeted me with a flashy smile.

'Hello, May. How are you?' I didn't have to ask. She was blooming. May had grown into an attractive young woman with sparkling eyes. Everything about her was clean and shining in a brassy sort of way. But to her credit she had made something of herself and now she was clearly bursting to tell me something.

'Saw Pete Scanlon the other night.' She was balancing a large bag of potatoes effortlessly on her knee.

'Oh really?'

'Who's the blonde he's with these days? I've seen her around but I don't know where she's from.'

She cast me a sidelong, malicious look, as she piled the sacks of potatoes neatly together in a corner.

'I've no idea. Two pounds of sugar please.' I licked my lips to conceal the dryness in my mouth.

It was when she was weighing out the sugar that I noticed the ring. It caught the shaft of sunlight from the open door and sparkled all the colours of the rainbow. Its brightness danced and winked before my eyes with May manoeuvring her hands around the blue sugar bag, filling it up in fine performance.

'How're things anyway?' she asked conversationally, removing her pencil from behind her ear to tot up the bill.

'Fine.'

'Any word from Vicky?'

'Yes. She seems to be bearing up in Canada.'

'She'll be back. Wait till you see. Thought of Ireland as her home.'

She twisted her ring with her thumb agitatedly while she waited for the money.

'Is that plaice fresh?'

'This mornin's.' She patted her curls with her left hand.

'Give me three fillets please.'

'That'll be sixpence.'

'You're very quiet.' She handed me my change.

'Anything on your mind? Or is it someone?' She put the emphasis on the 'someone'.

'Rubbish,' I laughed and escaped.

Mam was cheered up by the news that there was to be an increase in the gas allowance. From now on the gas would be on from 6.30 to 8.30 a.m. for breakfast, 11.30 to 2.00 p.m. and 5.30 to 7.00 p.m. Little things like that made all the difference to our bleak, uneventful lives.

Dad got me a part-time job working in the Home and Colonial. With my first week's wages I went to Dublin to shop with Tess. We bought Outdoor Girl make-up in their new 'Hollywood' red and pink and Cutex 'Lollipop' nail polish.

'Let's buy some of those stockings in Cassidy's in Georges Street,' said Tess.

We bought the new fine rayon hosiery for one and eleven pence a pair.

'There's a pretty frock. It's only two pounds and ten pence and I'd love it.' I tried to picture myself in it and wondered if Pete would like it too.

'Come on, try it on then.'

We spent an hour trying on frocks, with the shop assistant trying to entice us with a selection of pretty silk ones. I couldn't afford any of them.

'We take deposits,' she informed me.

I put a pound down on the one I'd seen in the window,

hoping that Mam would lend me the balance and somehow find ten spare coupons.

Times were still very hard and you couldn't shop without ration books. Even with them the ordinary working-class people found it difficult to make ends meet. Houses were scarce too. Although there were plans for an enormous new housing scheme in Dun Laoghaire, there was no money to start the building. Unemployment was high, food was scarce and choices limited.

'Anyone with a brain in their head is emigrating,' said Gran. 'I'd go meself only I'm too old.'

'You won't die of want here. Sure, aren't you comfortable enough?' Mam was annoyed.

'Very comfortable, Gertie, and grateful, but I'd like to make me own contribution to society.'

'Codswallop. Haven't you contributed enough? A whole family.'

'Hm.' Gran stopped talking.

One evening Pete drove up to our house in a second-hand Hillman and honked the horn until I came running to the door.

'Pete Scanlon, what's the matter with you? You'll waken the dead with that din,' Gran shouted at him.

Luckily Mam and Dad had gone to town for the day or some explaining would have had to be done. Dad hated any fuss and unnecessary noise.

'Get in. I'm taking you for a drive.'

He roared off down the road barely giving me time to slam the door shut.

'Well what do you think?' he asked again.

'It's terrific. Whose is it?'

'Mine,' he said proudly. 'You're my first passenger.'

'I'm honoured. Congratulations.'

He smiled with pure pleasure although he kept his eyes on the road. It was the old Pete Scanlon I sat beside. The Pete I first knew when we played Cowboys and Indians with the gang.

He parked in the car park at the seafront.

'Well what'd you think?'

'It's a gorgeous car. How many times do I have to tell you?'

'As often as you like,' he laughed.

It was black and smelt faintly of polish and leather.

'Good nick for a four-year-old.'

'How did you come by it?'

'Bought it as soon as it came into the garage. I told Mr Treacy to be on the lookout for something in good condition and he said I wouldn't do better than this for the money.'

He was happy and boyish again, the purchase of the car seeming to diminish his dreadful experiences of the war. His injuries were temporarily forgotten.

'It's paid for too. Every penny.'

'How did you manage that?'

'From my disability money. I can repair it myself, so

the running costs won't be much. Of course, when I'm fully trained I'll get something newer. Might even get a brand new car.'

There were only a few cars in Dun Laoghaire, and Pete looked out from the frame of the car window towards the horizon, proud behind his own steering wheel.

'It's a miracle how much progress you've made, Pete, since you've come home. I'm delighted for you.'

'Thanks.' He turned to me almost shyly.

'That must be why I haven't seen you. Busy organising this and working and everything?'

His eyes flickered but he said nothing for a minute.

'Well,' he flicked back his hair in a nervous gesture. 'It wasn't just that.'

'Oh?'

'It's sort of hard to explain. It's just that I don't want to get too involved with anyone yet.'

'What do you mean "too involved"?' I rounded on him.

'I don't want any commitments. Not when I'm just getting started and all . . .'

His face was flushed with embarrassment. He stared ahead not daring to look at me.

'Who's asking you to get involved? Certainly not me! I don't want a commitment from you or anyone else, Pete Scanlon, and get that straight. Anyway, you're probably still nursing a broken heart for Vicky.'

The words were out before I realised I'd said them.

'For Christ's sake, Lizzie Doyle, are you mad?'

He stared at me as if I'd lost my sanity. Knowing I'd gone too far, I turned away.

'What exactly is that remark supposed to mean?'

'Exactly what it says,' I answered, now furious myself and relieved in a distorted kind of way that I had mentioned Vicky. The painful past was out in the open at last, laid bare before us like an open wound.

'Do you really think I still carry a torch for Vicky?'

His face was stoney, his cheekbones as rigid as sculpture.

'What else am I supposed to think? You never mentioned her name since your return. After all, you were in England together.'

I was breathless.

'She followed me. I didn't invite her. No one was more surprised than me when she turned up.'

'You didn't exactly send her away.'

'Who says I didn't? She had no one else, only her stupid mother who was out all day. Anyway, when I was injured I couldn't cope with her mooning all over the hospital and crying . . .' His voice was edgy, the words clipped, and I knew he was telling me the truth. Vicky's letters had never mentioned that he was glad to see her. I'd gone too far.

'I'm sorry.'

'I should bloody well hope so. Next time get your

facts straight before you start assuming things.'

The tiredness had returned to his eyes as the tension mounted between us, and I cursed myself for putting him under unnecessary strain.

'I suppose it had to be said some time,' he conceded after a long silence.

'No. I shouldn't have said anything.'

'It was obviously on your mind.'

'Well yes. That time you went with Vicky you seemed to be mad about her.'

'I suppose I was at the time. I'm still fond of her. But we were only kids, for God's sake. The last thing I expected was that she'd chase after me.'

'Her father was putting pressure on her to go to Canada with him.' I spoke quickly. 'And she couldn't see any way out of it. She didn't want to go, so she ran away. The obvious place for her to go was to her mother and you. She missed you desperately, you know.'

'She told me.'

'Is that why you're afraid of a commitment? Are you afraid I'll be like Vicky and chase after you everywhere? Don't worry, Pete Scanlon, I won't.' I could feel my blood boil up inside.

'Temper, temper,' he laughed, defusing the situation. 'Apart from anything else, Vicky soon got tired of me when I got injured.'

I looked up into the tired face and my heart missed a beat.

'You don't have to swear undying love to me, Pete. We've been friends a long time. Why can't we just go on being friends? But I'm not a kid any more.'

His face softened.

'You think I don't know that?'

He leaned forward and traced the line of my lips with his, moving closer, kissing me with an urgency that was almost frightening.

'That's what I'm afraid of,' he whispered.

He gathered me into his arms and held me there. When he released me, his eyes were bright with desire.

'C'mon, let's go home.'

He drove to Sandycove and on to Dalkey along the Vico Road to Killiney, where Dublin Bay stretched out before us, twinkling in the dusk. He called it the long way home.

In spite of our agreement about no commitments and the fact that I only saw Pete casually during the summer, I was falling in love with him.

After a while I stopped trying to analyse every emotion. Hadn't I always loved Pete? I felt comfortable with him. I understood him. His loyalty to his drunken father, his pride through his hurt when he kicked him around. His arrogance as he strutted up and down the stage. The same arrogance he used as a defence mechanism against the hostility of his home environment and later at the front. His constant fear of failure since he was injured. A fear that drove him relentlessly to prove to himself and others that he could make something of himself. A fear that prevented him from wanting any responsibility for another human being.

He was only twenty-one years old, yet he had the mentality of man who'd lived far longer than that. I decided I would never become a burden on him, never let him know that I was in love with him in case he felt threatened.

He often called for me in his car and we would drive to the beach and walk hand in hand for miles and miles. Sometimes he took me to the Arcadia in Bray to dance to the music of Phil Murtagh and his resident band. May Tully had entered the 'Prettiest Girl' competition and she had managed to get to the finals. She desperately wanted to win the first prize of twenty pounds – a fortune – but proved a good loser when she came third and won a fiver.

Pete was developing a liking for dancing, in spite of his injured leg.

'It's good exercise,' he maintained.

'*When you're smiling,*' he sang along with the band, '*Keep on smiling.*' He had a beautiful rich, full voice. Phil Murtagh heard him sing and invited him to join the band. He was overjoyed.

'*It's all or nothing,*' he would sing, looking straight into my eyes and my mind flew back to the early days in the Workmen's Club in Dun Laoghaire. The dance usually closed to the bluesy notes of 'A Perfect Day' and 'It's All Over Now' sung by Phil himself and we would dance, clinging together to the rhythm of the music. Pete's singing career was launched. Apart from the confidence it inspired in him, we got free tickets to the Arcadia Ballroom every Saturday night.

'It's a great leg-up for him,' said Gran. 'If this doesn't get him out of himself, I don't know what will.'

'He's delighted. He can't believe he's getting paid for singing. He'd do it for nothing.'

'He always had a lovely voice, didn't he, Gertie?'

'Yes. That's one thing he did have.' Mam focused her attention on her knitting. I could feel the coldness in the air as if someone had left a door open.

We also danced in the Metropole in town. Sometimes we had our tea in the Grill Room early, before the dance began. Rashers, eggs, sausages, chips and a pot of tea with brown bread and butter. I savoured our time together, constantly reminding myself that Pete might disappear at any moment if he began to feel in the least bit claustrophobic.

He often called for me at the last minute, assuming I'd be available to go to the cinema or a dance. And I went.

We went to see *Odd Man Out*, with James Mason and Kathleen Ryan, and *The Jolson Story* with Larry Parks and Evelyn Keyes. Pete's car took us to places we could never have considered going to otherwise. Noel Purcell in Sean O'Casey's *Silver Tassie*, at the Gaiety. Dorothy

Maguire and Guy Madison in *Till the End of Time* at the Savoy.

Pete even invited Mam and Dad to see Ibsen's *Hedda Gabler* at the Gate. But Mam declined, with the excuse that they weren't in the best of form. Eighty-five-year-old Gran came instead. She dressed up in her best high-waisted dress, with a ruffled Irish lace collar. She carried her little black velvet bag entwined in her fingers, the mothballs intact.

'You're a smasher.' Pete took her arm and helped her into the car.

'Can it go faster?' she enquired and he put his foot down hard on the accelerator to impress her.

Dublin was swarming with Chinese sailors and Pete teased Gran for staring at them.

'I told you the country would be overrun with foreigners now the war's over. They've no place to go.'

'They must be hard up if they're coming here,' Pete laughed. 'Sure, isn't everyone leaving!'

Even as we discussed our separate futures, I knew I was becoming deeply involved with Pete in spite of all my promises to myself to keep my distance. Maybe our physical demonstrations were more poignant because of our continual threatened separation. Pete sometimes surprised me by the passion he unleashed in an unguarded moment. Then he would apologise and become tense and irritable like a coiled spring. I would wait for the mood to pass, pretending I hadn't even noticed.

Mostly being with him was pure joy. Watching the sunset from the top of the hill, counting the stars, making wishes when there was a new moon.

'Who would ever have thought of you and me here together like this?' Pete would say in wonder.

But I had thought of it. All the time.

We were at the Sailing Regatta, watching the yachts line up for the race.

'I have to go to England.' Pete was casual.

'England? Why?' I kept my eyes on the white sails ballooning in the wind.

'I'm being sent by the firm. I can tell you, I've no desire to go.'

'Is it promotion? How long will you be gone?'

This time I couldn't keep my voice steady.

'Only a couple of months. Bit of extra training they say. All expenses paid.'

'That's great. They must think a lot of you to invest in you like that.'

'I suppose.'

'When are you off?'

'Tomorrow.'

'Tomorrow!'

'Crack of dawn.'

'Oh.'

'Let's go.'

When we reached home Pete suggested a walk. The lane, still scorched from the day's heat, was brown and dusty. The grass and wild flowers were withered from the sun. Birds twittered and rustled in the trees, moving and settling for the night.

'You aren't upset or anything?' he asked.

'Of course not. I'm delighted for you,' I lied, looking up at the faint fretted stars of early evening. 'Just think, by the time you come back I'll have started nursing.'

He grinned. 'That's good. It'll keep you occupied. How do you like working in the shop?'

'It's all right. Bit difficult at times if a customer wants something we don't have.'

'I thought that shop sold everything.'

'Everything available. We're getting better stock in every day. I wish we didn't have to use the ration books still though. They're a nuisance.'

'You don't regret this summer? Spending so much time with me?'

'No.'

'I'll send a postcard.'

'Good.'

'You could always write back if I put the address on it.'

'Yes, I will.'

'I'd like that.'

'You'll take good care of yourself?'

'Of course, and you too.'

'Well I'm hardly likely to get injured this time. Unless I get run over by a bus or something stupid like that.'

He laughed and kept his eyes on our joined hands as the awkwardness grew between us. We continued walking in silence. The sun sank and we were cast in shadow.

'I hate goodbyes.' He looked away.

'Me too.'

'Then we won't say it.'

'Fine.'

We had reached the end. The magic of the lane was always a powerful elixir to me. The tall familiar trees stood guard like protective sentinels. The green field of unripe corn rippled in the evening breeze.

'I bet Mr Meaney is praying for a drop of rain.'

Pete wasn't listening. He was nervous and intent.

'You've helped me a lot, Lizzie, these past few months. I'm grateful.'

'I haven't done anything.' I shrugged, suddenly embarrassed.

'You have and you know it. You knew when to talk and when to leave me alone. You were there if I needed a bit of company or someone to take to the flicks.'

His words had a finality about them that I didn't like.

'It's great to see you getting on so well. You had the guts to get on with your life in spite of everything.'

He took me in his arms, the ancient gnarled apple tree giving us shelter.

'Thank you,' he said and kissed me slowly and tenderly. I longed to stay there for ever.

'I have to go.'

I blinked and smiled at him.

'Right. See you.'

He looked at me for a moment then turned to go.

'Pete?'

'Yes?'

He waited. I stared at him helplessly. I wanted to say 'Don't go' but knew if I did I might ruin my chances of ever seeing him again. The risk was too great. Still I was desperate to hold him there.

'What?' He came back and stood beside me.

'Nothing.'

He smiled an understanding smile.

'Just take care of yourself, that's all.'

'Don't worry, I will.'

'So long.' He walked away, swift and assured, the walking stick long dispensed with. Pete Scanlon was ready to take on the world again.

I picked a dandelion clock and twirled it between my fingers, watching its tiny seed heads float away, and wondered where I fitted into this new-found confidence of his. Or if I did at all.

'Are you all right?' Mam's eyes were fixed on the skeleton of the dandelion.

'Yes thanks.'

Dad was listening to a play on the wireless. The play

ended with the song 'It's a long way to Tipperary', and Dad switched it off.

'Was that about the war?' I asked, attempting to divert Mam's attention.

'Yes. Same old thing all the time.'

'Like a cup of tea?' Mam asked.

'I'll put the kettle on.' I went to the sink.

'Not for me thanks. I'm off to bed. Goodnight.'

Dad left the kitchen.

'Pete getting on well in his job?' said Mam, doggedly pursuing the conversation.

'Fine.'

'He's looking well. It's good to see him back to his old self again. He was so thin when he first came home. I suppose we can't even conceive what the war was really like. Not even in our wildest dreams. Only people who were there . . .'

'No.'

'You're falling in love with him.' Her eyes never left my face while she waited for me to speak.

Our eyes met and my vision blurred as I lowered my head. She drew in her breath, shaking her head at the same time.

'Karen started romancing too young. Look what happened to her. Her life was ruined. I don't want to see you make the same mistake, Lizzie.'

She spoke casually enough but her eyes held a wariness in them.

'That won't happen. You don't have to worry.'

'I sincerely hope not. All that trouble . . .'

I stared out the kitchen window at the leaves and papers swirling about in the rising wind and shivered with sudden cold.

'I'll be sensible.'

'Pete Scanlon has had it hard. Bound to have problems.'

We sipped our tea in easy silence, my mind full of Pete, hers full of John and Karen and their future.

Her shoulders had lost their broadness. The weight of her troubles seemed to have diminished her in some way. Karen's sorrow had taken its toll and eaten at her very soul. I vowed there and then never to cause her any grief.

'Thanks, Mam.'

'For what?'

'For the tea, and for not giving me a lecture.'

I hugged her quickly and left, afraid I might break down and confide too much in her. Anyway there was really nothing to tell.

'She doesn't want to see you get hurt, Lizzie. That's all,' said Gran when I told her I didn't think Mam approved of Pete.

The postcard arrived a couple of weeks later.

Weather fairly good. Some rain. Working hard.
   Take good care.
   Pete

I read the straight neat handwriting over and over looking for some secret message or code. There was none. But it brought him back to life in my mind and into the room. Warm, wild, and passionate Pete who forced me out of my romantic dream world and into the reality of things.

Devon

The biggest surprise was a short note from Pete inviting me to join him for a few days in London.

I'll be here longer than I expected to be. Would like you to join me for a few days?
  Pete

A sinking feeling followed quickly on the heels of my immediate euphoric reaction. Mam would never let me go. To go away with a man unchaperoned was tantamount to being a fallen woman in her eyes. I wondered how to broach the subject but couldn't come up with a good enough reason for wanting to go to London. Auntie Sissy certainly wasn't on her list of favourite people. If only Vicky were there, then I would have the pretext of seeing her again.

After all my agonising, the permission was granted without much trouble. Pauline Byrne was going on holidays to London to her cousin and I casually mentioned to Mam that I'd love to go with her just for a few days.

'You could do with a break. Where will you stay?'

'Pauline has invited me.'

I had never deliberately deceived Mam but I was desperate to escape and desperate to see Pete again. She'd been thinking more in terms of Uncle Mike's for a holiday for me.

'London would be an education I suppose,' was all she said.

The boat, for all its gleaming countenance, was dirty; the train journey from Holyhead to London long and tiring. London was grimy, with huge gap-toothed spaces where houses had been. There were broken roofs and half houses exposing their insides, bits of curtain still blowing in the wind. Rebuilding was in progress but the gaps were a testimony to the war and the terrible havoc it had wrought. Arrows still pointed to air raid shelters. Pipes lay strewn along roads. Building sites were everywhere. London could only be observed behind high scaffoldings and people went about their business quietly, weary and disillusioned after their terrifying experiences. In some areas whole streets were missing.

Euston Station was cold, dingy and war-scarred. I shivered, my eyes scanning the crowd for Pete. He was beside me taking my arm firmly.

'Hello.' He kissed me on the cheek, his face reddening with embarrassment.

'You're soaked through,' I was trying to hide my own embarrassment.

There were wet patches on his shoulders and the rain had turned his fair hair a shade darker. But his face was wreathed in smiles as he took my hand and led me to the Underground self-assuredly, with hardly a trace of a limp.

I was glad I'd come.

The Underground was hot and uncomfortable. We stood close together in the packed carriage oblivious to the jostlings of our fellow travellers. The stations were still badly lit as if the Londoners were afraid that the war would erupt again if they illuminated the way for the enemy.

I was tired and glad of Pete's arm gripped tightly around my waist. By the time we reached our destination it was dark and cold. He carried my suitcase as we walked along a maze of suburban roads to his digs.

He turned the key in the lock. 'Sorry I can't carry you over the threshold but Mrs Cartwright wouldn't approve.'

'Neither would I.'

The digs were the biggest surprise. Brightly lit and welcoming with a burning fire in the grate. The dining-room table was beautifully laid for two.

Mrs Cartwright, his landlady, hurried in, large and brisk with blue eyes that warmed when she smiled.

'Pleased to meet you I'm sure,' she said. 'Would you like me to show you to your room? You might like to wash. You look frozen.'

'Yes. I'd like that.'

She led the way upstairs, her ample rump swaying

with each step. I was led down a long corridor smelling of polish and Brasso to a tiny room at the end.

'Make yourself comfortable. Bathroom on the left and I won't make the tea until you come downstairs.'

She turned the full curiosity of her gaze on me.

'Pete's room is down the far end. No corridor-hopping in the night. Against the rules.'

The smile took the sting out of her words of warning but didn't reach her steely eyes.

I shivered as I sat down on the soft feather bed. The flower-sprigged curtains and counterpane were fresh and clean and bright rugs lay scattered on the highly polished floor. Suddenly I was reminded of Sister Stella Maris and school. Knowing Pete was waiting anxiously for me downstairs bucked me up and I hurried down to join him.

'Guess what she said?' I whispered when we were alone.

'What?'

'She said no corridor-hopping. How could she even think such a thing? It took me several minutes to work out what she meant.'

Pete laughed.

'You should see your face!'

He was watching me with that expression in his eyes that made me want to ignore Mrs Cartwright and the tea she was pouring. I would have gladly forsaken her tea for us to be alone, in each other's arms. I returned his gaze, knowing with certainty that he knew what I was thinking.

'Corridor-hopping mightn't have crossed your mind but it certainly crossed mine.'

We were finishing our tea and whispering like a couple of schoolchildren.

'Pete Scanlon, how could you say such a thing? If you think I'm that sort of girl you can forget it. I'll go and pack and leave instantly.'

'Calm down. I said it crossed my mind. I didn't say . . .' He was laughing so much he couldn't finish the sentence. 'Anyway, don't worry about her rules and regulations. It's only for tonight. Tomorrow we're off and you won't see her again.'

'Off where?'

'God knows! Wherever the fancy takes us. I've a loan of a car and a full tank of petrol so who knows where we might end up. Come on, finish your tea, we have a busy day ahead of us tomorrow.'

I lay between fresh sheets that smelled of lavender and thought of Pete and that secretive look in his eyes when he mentioned setting off tomorrow on the mystery tour he'd planned. Were his intentions strictly honourable? I somehow doubted it. Did he consider me loose and immoral like the floozie Mrs Keogh's husband went off with? I didn't know. I didn't really know much about Pete's intentions at all and hadn't tried to find out. I was so delighted to have been asked I forgot to consider the reasons. Pete was an enigma. For all the laughing, mischievous side of him, there was the darker, mysterious element intangible to me. Anyway, tomorrow would reveal his secrets. I fell fast asleep.

Pete drove confidently, heading south through the English countryside that lay warm and hazy in the late summer sun. We drove through sun-dappled roads, past miles of hedgerows, distancing ourselves from London as fast as we could go, only stopping for a cup of tea and a sandwich.

'I've just one thing to do on the way. I want to place a bet. There's a great little filly running at Doncaster. Can't lose.'

'You're still keen on the horses?' I'd forgotten how much Pete frequented the bookies in Dun Laoghaire.

'Just the odd flutter. When I'm guaranteed to win.' And he went off to find a betting shop.

The countryside drowsed as we roared past. In the late evening we arrived at our destination, a tiny village called Bude on the Devonshire coast. The reflection of the setting sun shimmered on the sea as the bay curved around corkscrew bends expertly negotiated by Pete.

We stopped outside a picture postcard thatched cottage, where late roses rambled round the door, and a sign swung in the evening breeze confirming that we had arrived at our destination, the Rose and Crown Tavern.

We hauled in our bags. Polished brass and wood glinted welcomingly as we checked into the bar.

'Would you like a drink?'

'I'd love a cup of tea.'

'Certainly.' The barman disappeared behind a curtain.

'This is cosy.' Pete looked pleased.

'Dinner's at eight.' The barman returned with a tray. 'I hope your stay will be comfortable.'

The bedrooms, large and airy, were side by side.

'No need for "corridor-hopping" here,' Pete laughed.

'Don't go getting any ideas either,' I warned and went to change into my floral print frock, and comb my hair.

After a delicious dinner, where shortages and ration books seemed to be unheard of, we went for a walk. We walked through narrow lanes and climbed a hill past an old churchyard. At the top we watched the fishing boats sail home and drop anchor to deliver their day's catch.

'It's heaven.' I breathed in the salt sea air, closing my eyes, my arm resting on Pete's.

'With my eyes closed like this it's easy to imagine I'm dreaming,' I told him.

I pushed back my windblown hair. Pete was looking at me.

'Was it difficult to get away?'

'Not really but then I didn't say exactly where I was going.'

'How could you? You didn't know exactly where you were going.'

'You know what I mean.'

'Any regrets?'

'Not so far. Why did you decide to bring me here?'

'I missed you.'

'It's costly.'

He shrugged. 'That's not important. The fact that you're here is important. It's the most important thing right now.'

I looked at him in astonishment.

'I thought your job was the most important thing in your life.'

'So did I until I discovered what cold comfort a lump of metal is, compared to . . .'

'Compared to?' I prompted.

'Compared to you.' He leaned against a boulder, his blue eyes intent on me. 'I suppose what I'm trying to say is that I love you.'

We faced one another. His eyes were moist and his face was rigid again. No one could have looked less like a man in love.

'Why is it so difficult?'

He pulled me to him, stifling tears, and held me without a word for what seemed to be for ever.

'It's just that I feel I have so little to offer you. I'm just a wounded old soldier.'

'You can't mean that.'

'I've worked hard to get experience and get promotion. I wanted to have something worthwhile to offer you before I asked you to marry me.' He looked away. 'I didn't allow for the loneliness.'

'Oh Pete.'

'I love you, Lizzie. I love you very much indeed. I think I always have.'

He pulled me down beside him, kissing me, holding me tight.

'You're beautiful,' he said, releasing me to gaze into my eyes.

Then slowly his hands moved over my body. Touching, exploring, without any resistance from me. Only the hoot of a distant owl broke the silence. Suddenly we were overpowered by an emotion too strong for either of us to resist.

'I've wanted you for so long,' he whispered hoarsely and I pulled him to me, returning his kisses with an urgency to match his own. But when he finally entered me it hurt. So much that I cried out and he stopped the slow rhythm and pulled away.

'I'm sorry, Lizzie.' He stroked my hair and gently kissed me. 'I didn't think . . . too greedy for you . . . Can you ever forgive me?'

'Don't say anything,' I said a while later.

We were silent for a long time. My blatant desire for him had frightened me more than anything else. He knew it too. That night he came to my room. We lay side by side talking casually and when he finally made love to me I responded eagerly. There was no pain this time, only exquisite pleasure.

'I love you,' I told him before he left my room but I couldn't sleep, racked with guilt for what I'd just done. I thought of Mam and Dad. What if I were to get pregnant like Karen had? Shame washed over me, extinguishing my happiness. I could hardly face Pete next morning.

As we drove back to London and Euston station I saw the intensity in Pete's eyes. His whole demeanour was tense. He hardly spoke. He held me tight as we said our goodbyes but his words of love were not repeated.

I had waited years it seemed to hear the words that he'd said but instead of feeling the lightness of a weight lifted from me I felt their burden hovering somewhere in the vicinity of my heart.

Back home, Gran met me at the door.

'Well?' She hugged me like a returned immigrant. 'Did you enjoy yourself?'

I could hardly meet her penetrating gaze.

'Yes thanks, Gran. It's a long journey though.'

'Here, give me your things and go up and see your Mam. She's in bed.'

'Is she sick?' My heart flipped over.

'No. Nothing like that. Just a bit tired.'

'What's wrong, Mam?' I hugged her tight.

'Just having a rest.' She looked pale and gaunt as she lay propped up with pillows. 'I'll come down and get you something to eat in a minute. How was your holiday?'

'Great. Don't stir. I can get something for myself. How's everything? Any word from Karen?'

Mam sighed and turned her face into the pillow.

'She rang yesterday. She's staying another while in North Carolina. She says Paul's parents are insisting on it because John is having such a wonderful time.'

'That's good news, isn't it?'

'The reason she's staying on has nothing to do with John. She's just using him as an excuse. So I got cross.'

'Oh Mam. Aren't you being a bit harsh?'

'Am I? Whatever else, I'm not going senile, Lizzie. That girl has fallen for Paul's cousin. I know it.'

'Wouldn't it be wonderful if she were to find happiness again, Mam? Isn't that what you and Dad want most for her? A fresh start.'

'Not in America. She's neglected to consider our feelings. After all, we've reared John since she left him and went back to England. Didn't she think we'd get attached to him? She's acting irresponsibly and I'm not sure she's fit to choose a husband.'

'Mam!'

I couldn't believe my ears. Not once in all my life did I ever remember hearing Mam criticise Karen. Not even when she was pregnant with John.

'Well, I'm speaking my mind for once. You're old enough now to understand. God knows, it's all been festering for so long. Extending her holiday is the last straw. I boiled over on the phone and got an earful of abuse in return. I wish we'd never had that phone installed. I'll ask Bill to have it disconnected.'

'They'll be back soon and you can discuss it together then.'

'I suppose so. I just hope she doesn't do anything foolish.'

'Like what?'

'Like take a notion and marry him.'

'She won't. She'll come home first.'

'I wish I could believe you. Anyway, I didn't mean to dwell on Karen. Sit down and tell me all about you. Where did you go? Who did you meet?'

'London was wonderful. Of course . . . it's devastated still.'

There was silence while Mam waited to hear more. Then she looked sharply at me. 'How was Pete Scanlon?'

The question was so unexpected that I dropped the cushion I was fiddling with.

'How did you know I saw Pete?'

'His mother told me. You should have told me yourself.'

'I didn't want to worry you.'

'Well I was twice as worried when I had to hear it from her. Pete's not the one for you, Lizzie. This time I'm not going to sit back and let things happen the way I did with Karen. Pete's got a lot of problems. Can't be relied upon.'

'Mam!' I was shocked.

'Apart from anything else, he's a gambler and don't

you deny it. His mother told me ages ago that he spent his whole day practically in the bookies.'

'That was when he first came home and had nothing to do. Pete is very ambitious. He works hard and saves. How else could he afford to treat me to such an expensive holiday?'

'Probably had a bit of a windfall with the horses. I hope his intentions were honourable, Lizzie?'

I turned away from her disapproving eyes. She sighed and looked sad. The weight of her sadness was more apparent as she lay there thinking.

'When you eventually get married I hope it'll be to a good, solid man with a reliable job. Someone who'll look after you.'

'Pete has a good job . . .' My voice trailed away.

There was no use arguing with her. Not when she was in this mood.

'I'll go and put the kettle on.' I left the room.

Gran and I sat in the kitchen drinking tea.

'Mam says Pete's a gambler, Gran, but he only backs the horses when he's sure of a winner.'

Gran understood.

'You know I like a flutter meself,' she said. 'I often put a shilling each way on one of me favourites.' She whistled through her false teeth as she nodded her head in satisfaction. 'That time I was sick and couldn't get out to back a horse, it nearly killed me.'

'I would have done it for you.'

'You or Vicky in the bookies at that age! The idea!'

She sighed, a look of martyrdom on her face, conveniently forgetting all the times she had sent us to the pub for a Baby Power.

'Now with me old age pension no one can stop me. Sure, when me horse romps home there's no pleasure in the wide world like it.'

Mam came in in her dressing-gown and sat down.

'Gran spends more time in the bookies these days than she does in the church.' There was a tremor of annoyance in her voice.

'Don't exaggerate, Gertie.' Gran was used to criticism that assumed she was doing more of something than she really was.

'I'm off to bed.' She took the paper and left.

'She takes the paper from your dad to study form. He's lucky to get a look at it. She commandeers the wireless just to listen to the racing. We haven't a minute's peace with her. It's not good for Dad's blood pressure.'

'I didn't know she was that bad.'

'She's gone to the dogs altogether lately. Doesn't even bother to hide her affliction.'

'It's hardly an affliction at her age, Mam. Sure, she has very few pleasures in life.'

'More than I have. Though she's eased off on the drink. It doesn't agree with her any more. We've that to be grateful for at least. But she's a bad loser. Goes around cursing the bloody fool of a horse for hours.' Her annoyance was now focused on Gran and I was grateful for the reprieve.

I knew she'd eventually get back to the subject of Pete Scanlon. It came sooner than I thought.

The following Saturday I had a half-day and stayed in to wash my hair. We were listening to the sponsored programmes on the wireless when Gran suddenly switched over to the Fairyhouse races and began leaping out of her chair and shouting at the poor unfortunate horse she had backed.

'Come on, ye lazy strap. Move those legs will ye?' she yelled, shaking her fist at the wireless.

'You've no shame, Gran.' Mam eyed her disapprovingly. 'Doesn't even try to hide her obsession with those bloody horses.' This remark was addressed to me. Gran didn't even hear her. She was too busy cursing the horse, the jockey, the state of the course, the trainer.

'It's the thrill of it.' She finally sat back to draw breath when the race was over.

'I wouldn't hold it against poor Pete Scanlon if he likes a bet once in a while. He's had it tough.'

Mam's eyes blazed at me.

'You're starting your nurses' training course in St. Michael's on 1 September. I've filled in the forms and sent the hundred pounds. You'll be living in, so that'll put a stop to your gallop.' She delivered the information like a terse news bulletin. Gran whistled through her teeth but said nothing.

'Won't I have an interview?'

'In due course. But Mother Attracta assures me she'll keep a place for you. I've sent on your Leaving Certificate results.'

'It pays to keep in with the nuns.' Gran resumed her knitting. 'I'll knit you a white cardigan, Lizzie. Them oul' corridors are very cold. You won't be far from home. Not like that oul' boarding school.' She was trying to comfort herself as much as me.

'I can't wait.' I looked defiantly at Mam.

'You won't be hopping home every five minutes. Or running around the town either. They're very strict.'

'I'll get time off, won't I? Even a criminal gets time off for good behaviour.'

'None of your cheek.'

She sealed her lips, drawing the conversation to a close.

Every time she thought I was getting too close to Pete Scanlon for her liking she drove a wedge between us. This time it was a whole scaffolding. She might as well put me in prison and throw away the key, so determined was she to keep me out of his reach. When she was that determined she usually succeeded. I longed to be a nurse, so I minded less than she thought.

'Psstt, Lizzie, put five bob on Jumpin' Jack. He's running in the three o'clock at Newbury. I've got a hunch.' I laughed but Gran was deadly serious.

'Mam's right. You've gone to the dogs.'

'Ah, don't mind her. She's lost without John and it's getting her down. Now listen. This is a grand little stallion.' She put the money into my hand, her old face creased in millions of wrinkles.

'Here's a few bob for yourself, girl. Get a pair of them new stockings.'

'Nylons, you mean?'

'The very ones. And don't say a word to your Mam or Dad. No use upsetting them. Sure, you know I can take or leave the oul' horses.'

Gran went down to McCullough's to put a deposit on the wool for my cardigan. Mam accompanied her in case she fell. She was getting frail.

'She still doesn't trust me,' Gran complained to me.

'She does. She's just afraid you'll fall.'

'Listen, Lizzie, it'll work out all right,' she whispered. 'Give it time. You're young and lovely and he's a decent lad. I don't think he'd ever want to hurt you intentionally. Your mam and dad are so worried about Karen. Don't have them worried about you as well.'

It took me a few seconds to realise that Gran was talking about Pete Scanlon. Lately she'd started speaking out on whatever preyed on her mind. But she was tactful.

'You're an angel, Gran. Don't be worried about me. I've hardly given Pete Scanlon a second thought since I came home.'

'Good.' She was satisfied with that answer and went off to set the table.

It was a lie. I had thought of little else.

Vicky

The mist rolled in from the sea, thick moisture gathering and dispersing with the tide. It was the beginning of winter and the fresh sunlit mornings had given way to fog. From the hospital window I watched the rolling sea, the screeching gulls, and the mailboat as it waited, slick and sleek, to sound its hooter and be ready for the off. All familiar sights to me. Even the lurching pain in my heart was no stranger. Pete Scanlon was taking that very boat back to England for good.

'There's nothing here for me.' His features were immobile, his eyes red-rimmed and fiery. We were sitting in his kitchen after his mother's funeral. She had died suddenly on her way home from mass one morning.

'Just dropped, poor woman,' sniffed Gran. 'She'd had enough of the hardship. A saint, that woman was. A real saint.'

'What about us?' I looked at Pete, mortified that I should have to be the one to pose the question.

He shrugged. 'You know where I am if you want me. It's up to you.'

His indifference stabbed me and accelerated the guilt I'd felt ever since our weekend in Devon.

'I have to finish my training.'

'That's more important?' The question was loaded.

'At the moment, yes.'

'That's it then, isn't it?' He lit a cigarette and watched me through a smoke-screen. 'I was never good enough for you. You were always beyond my reach. Your mother saw to that. Wasn't I the fool to think we'd ever get together?' His voice trailed away.

'We got together in Devon.'

'Much good that did. You acting the martyr. You'd think I'd committed a crime. It was only one night.'

'Oh really? Is that all it meant to you? A one-night stand?'

'I didn't mean that.'

'Oh no. Then you had nothing to lose. I lost my virginity and could have ended up pregnant into the bargain.'

'If your virginity was so precious, why did you bother? I didn't force myself on you. Though God knows you acted as if I did afterwards.'

'You're the one acting the martyr. Ever since the bloody war . . .'

'I'm going. Goodbye.'

I hadn't seen him since.

It was three months since I'd walked into the imposing

red-bricked hospital to begin my training. Three months of scrubbing floors and washing bilious green walls, emptying bed pans, cleaning sluices and doing everything except actually nursing a patient.

Hygiene was preached to us from morning till night. Damp-dusting the wards and making beds with hospital corners seemed to take precedence over the patients. I was anxious to get down to do the job I had come to train for. Nursing.

Sister Louise was our Sister-in-charge.

'Practice makes perfect,' she repeated over and over.

I didn't believe her. Would I ever become proficient in even the most menial tasks? The helpless patients posed a threat in those interminable first days. I dashed around catching up on all my chores while skilled nurses took it all in their stride.

'You'll get the hang of it,' Staff Sister said, as she marched me from bed to bed, inspecting patients with her eagle eye.

'Wash number five. Change that dressing. Take that temperature,' she muttered through clenched teeth.

'How are you today, Mrs Smith? Bowels move yet?' She smiled sweetly at the red-faced woman in the bed.

'Not yet. Still on the dresser,' Mrs Smith quipped.

'I'll order more prunes.' Staff laughed her artificial laugh. 'It's a wonder she doesn't explode,' she sighed moving on.

It was the same performance every morning.

★ ★ ★

Matron was a neat little nun who terrified us with her weekly inspection. She was as severe as she was fastidious. No task was too great or too small for us, provided it was menial. Yet, as the chores became routine, my confidence grew.

We were lectured in hygiene, anatomy and physiology and were expected to study in what little spare time we had. The rules of the hospital specified that every trainee nurse must live in. I went home on Wednesdays. My half-day. Gran always made a fuss of me.

'Take the weight off your feet,' she'd say with reverence. 'Did I tell you about the pain in me big toe, Lizzie?' She'd remove her thick stocking to stretch out a lumpy foot in front of me. 'I'm slowing down. Can hardly move some days with the pains in me oul' bones.'

She was irritated by her increasing lack of mobility, afraid she'd one day be imprisoned in her bed. So she made valiant efforts to 'keep going'. She slept in her chair more, her eyes sunken in her head. But she was in good spirits.

'Here, put a few bob on this one,' she'd say, slipping me a bit of paper with the money wrapped up in it. 'The divil take him if he doesn't clear them all.' And she'd shake her walking stick in the air. Gran always put her false teeth in for the race so she could grind them at the horses and jockeys.

One day Mam was outside the hospital waiting for me as I came off duty.

'May Tully's getting married. She's sent an invitation to you and Vicky.'

'Is it that actor fellow?'

'Yes. Seems they're off to Hollywood.'

'Hollywood!' I exploded.

'Apparently the whole cast from the Abbey are signing contracts for some film.'

May Tully a film star! Who would have believed it? She'd done well since she went to train in the Abbey. But a film star, that was something else.

'It was nice of her to remember Vicky all the same.'

'She won't come. Not all the way from Canada. Even if May is a film star.' We laughed and went shopping.

I couldn't have been more wrong. Two days before May's wedding, Staff sent for me.

'You have a visitor.'

'Is something wrong?'

'I don't think so. We don't encourage visitors. Don't be long.'

I hurried down the corridor to Reception expecting to find Mam or Dad, or Karen, or even Pete. Pete? My heart beat wildly against my rib cage, slowing me down as I fought to control my nervousness. Could there be something wrong with Karen? John? Oh no. Not John.

'Hello, Lizzie.'

233

She was tall and slim in a narrow, belted coat. Her black hair hung to her shoulders and her clear dark eyes held love in their intensity.

'Vicky!'

We hugged each other, tears spilling uncontrollably down my face. I wanted to say so much, ask so many questions, but I couldn't form the words. Vicky was smiling and composed.

'Oh, Lizzie, you are a softie. Here quick, dry your eyes.'

I took the tiny handkerchief she proffered and dabbed at my eyes.

'How . . . ? When . . . ? Why . . . ?' We burst out laughing and sat down to gaze at one another.

'May's wedding gave me the cattle prod I needed. I've been dying to come home and I guess this is as good a time as any.' She spoke with a languid Canadian twang.

'Oh Vicky, it's wonderful to see you. I've missed you so much.'

'I've missed you and everyone else too. You look so funny in that uniform.'

She laughed and traces of the old Vicky returned. But she was so sophisticated, so beautiful. I expected to wake up any minute and find I was dreaming.

'How's Pete?'

'He's in England now.'

For a moment my heart lurched and my old enemy,

that deadly sin envy, returned. Would Pete fancy her if he saw her now? She certainly was fanciable.

'When did you arrive?'

'Late last night. I thought I'd surprise you first thing.'

'You certainly did that.'

'You'd better get back on duty. Your mam's ringing to ask if you can have a little time off. Compassionate leave or something.'

'Oh no. Staff'll kill me.'

'No she won't. I'll be waiting. Hurry home.'

That day I raced home on my old bike, still wondering if I'd been dreaming. But sure enough Vicky was there, settled in as if she'd never left. I swapped my day off with Mary Driscoll, my room mate, so there was no problem about staying out.

'How's Uncle Hermy and Auntie Sissy?'

'Much the same. They go their separate ways these days. Mum's involved in her charity work and Dad, well, God only knows what he's involved in. Which reminds me, he wants me to collect the suitcase he left here.'

'Suitcase? What suitcase?'

'He gave it to Aunt Gertie to mind. She'll know.'

'Oh that little case. I remember now. The one Gran thought had a wireless set in it.'

'Oh God! Just imagine Gran reporting him to the police. It's too much,' she cried, between helpless peals of laughter.

'She thought if she got him locked up in jail she

could keep you here for ever. It was the only solution in her eyes. She knew you didn't want to go to Canada.'

'She didn't want me to go either. Poor Gran.'

'Less of your poor Gran.' Gran came stiffly into the room, leaning heavily on her walking stick. 'Isn't it good to see the two of you together. Like old times.' She feasted her eyes on Vicky.

'And such a swank. With your posh Canadian accent. Here, give your old gran another hug. I'm off to bed.' Vicky hugged her. 'Praise the Lord for sparing me to see you again.' Tears misted the tired eyes that gazed lovingly into Vicky's.

'You'll see plenty of me, Gran. I'll be home often to tend to your creaking bones.'

'Which reminds me . . .' Gran started and Vicky burst into fresh peals of laughter.

'I'll give you a thorough examination first thing in the morning.'

'Right,' Gran said and clumped off upstairs.

'You've made an old woman very happy, Vicky. What more could she want with a medical student and a nurse to tend to her every whim!'

'It's what she deserves. I wish I were fully qualified. She'd be so proud.'

'She is proud. Can't you see it in her eyes?'

'Yes.'

Vicky looked thoughtful.

'Wasn't it lucky for me in a way there was a war? Otherwise I'd never have known Gran properly. Or had a proper family life with you all. Those were my happiest years.'

'You must be the only one in the world who benefited from the war, Vicky.'

'Well, one of the few anyway,' she agreed.

Mam found the suitcase she'd hidden for Uncle Hermy.

'I'm going to open it,' Vicky declared. 'Just to prove Gran wrong.'

'It's got clothes in it. I told her that. It's not heavy enough for a wireless set.'

She was trying to prise the tiny lock open with a pair of scissors.

'You'll damage it. Here's a pair of tweezers.'

'I told you it was clothes.' I surveyed the faded looking vest that was revealed when the lock finally shot back and the lid of the case flew open.

'Why was he so anxious to get it back?' Vicky was perplexed. 'I could have sworn he only agreed to let me come so I could collect this case,' she said, lifting out the bundle of old clothes. As she unravelled the underwear an enormous brown parcel fell heavily to the floor.

'Hardly a wireless. Quick, what is it?'

'Patience. It's glued together tightly and the paper's thick.' She reached for the scissors when she couldn't tear it open with her fingers.

'Oh be careful. Don't hack it. There might be some valuable secret documents there. Cut near the edge.'

'Hang on.'

She cut slowly along the edge of the parcel for what seemed an age before she pulled out an old yellowish faded parcel.

'Not another one.'

As she tore its flimsy paper wide open, five and ten pound notes fell like leaves to the floor.

'Look!' Vicky screeched.

'My God!'

There was an endless amount. There were more in another flatter parcel at the bottom of the case.

'Have you ever seen so much money in your life?'

Vicky's eyes were round with amazement as she sat among the money littering the floor.

'No, never. Not even in the shop when they were counting the end of the day's takings. No wonder Uncle Hermy was anxious to get his case back.'

'Just think what we could have done with it all these years.'

'Beautifully pressed, too. Do you think he ironed them before he packed them away?'

'Wouldn't be surprised. Now let's count it all. I wonder if it's legal tender still?'

'Of course it is. But you'll have to go to the bank to declare it. They'll never let you take it out of the country.'

'Who won't?'

'The authorities. Better ask Dad.'

'No. Say nothing. I'll pack it all away, and put it through my luggage.'

'That's too risky. They might think you robbed a bank and arrest you.'

'Shh! Keep your voice down. Here's what we'll do. We'll spend some, so there'll be less to carry and more clothes to wrap the rest up in.'

Vicky's eyes shone with excitement, just as they used to when she was engrossed in a scheme with May Tully.

'This is deadly serious. It's not a game. Your dad will have a fit if you spend any of that money.'

'No he won't. He'll be so pleased to get most of it back after all this time that he'll realise he's lucky. Supposing the house had caught fire or Auntie Gertie had spent it?'

'She wouldn't. He knew that when he asked her to mind it.'

'Here, you count this lot. Let's start.' Vicky began to hum. 'Well, little Lizzie, we'll sure knock 'em dead at this wedding. We're off to Dublin tomorrow.'

'I can't. I'm working,' I wailed.

'Never mind. Trust me. I'll get you something really special.'

May Tully marched her new husband triumphantly down the aisle to the fanfare of the organ and church bells and cheering guests. May looked like a film star already, in a hat of stiffened chiffon to match her frock, and tied in a lace bow under her chin.

The aquamarine silk frock Vicky had bought me hugged my body like a second skin. I wondered what Uncle Hermy would say if he could see me standing there in purest silk with matching coat and pillbox hat, purchased with his money. Vicky's taste proved impeccable and expensive. She wore a cream linen costume that accentuated her dark colouring and creamy complexion.

The word had spread like wildfire that May was almost a film star and all the 'gang' were there. To my amazement I saw Pete Scanlon among them and ignored him.

'When did Pete come home?' I asked Jimmy casually.

'Late last night. He's only here for the wedding. Going back tomorrow.'

We posed for endless photographs with May, who was as possessive of Vicky as she was of her man.

'Isn't he gorgeous?' she trilled, smiling at the thin boy-man who stood tousle-haired and shy at her side.

'Just one more for the album,' the photographer called, and Mrs Tully moved in for the kill.

'Everyone straighten up and stand close together,' she commanded, pushing her little husband into the row behind her.

The photographer took pictures of May posing and pouting against the backdrop of the magnificent gardens of the Royal Marine Hotel. The sunshine obliged for half an hour and then the heavens opened.

'Wouldn't you think we had enough rain all the month of August without more of it?' said Mrs Keogh, shielding her new purple felt hat inadequately with her handbag.

The hot soup at the hotel calmed the frayed nerves of the guests.

'This cost a pretty penny,' Pete said surveying the sumptuous spread laid out under the chandeliers. I ignored him again.

'Lizzie,' he called. I turned away.

'They had the turkeys flown in specially, I believe.' Mrs Keogh was her usual fund of information.

'Flew up from the country themselves, you mean. I thought May would be more partial to a bit of goose,' Jimmy Scanlon sniggered.

'Shut your mouth. Can't take you anywhere,' his father hissed across the table at him. For once he himself was presentable.

'I hear he's courtin'.' Mrs Keogh stopped chewing.

'Well you heard wrong,' Pete Scanlon turned on her. 'You always were a nosey oul' bag.'

'How dare . . .'

'Beautiful chandeliers. I'd hate to have to polish them,' Mrs Tully called over. 'But you're the expert in that department, Mrs Keogh.'

'I don't like heights,' she replied indignantly and continued eating, still smarting from Pete's rebuke.

'May's been saving up for this since she was born. Hasn't she, Vicky?' Jimmy Scanlon gave Vicky a meaningful look.

'How would I know?' said Vicky innocently.

''Course you'd know. Weren't you saving with her?'

'Well, she's certainly pushed the boat out good and proper,' said Mam. 'It's a lovely spread. Such a beautiful hotel too.'

'Will I cut your meat, Gran?' Vicky asked.

'Certainly not.' Gran was indignant, although she found it difficult to eat with her new set of dentures. 'They'll be all right when I've broken them in. Ornaments is all they are. I think I'll take them out.'

'No you won't,' Mam snapped.

'All right, Gertie. Calm down. Have a drop of champagne. I can recommend it.' Gran took a sip and her stomach gurgled. Her nose turned red as a beacon. Mam threw her eyes up to heaven. Gran's body went into a spasm of hiccuping.

'Gran!' Mam hissed at her.

'What's wrong with you now? I'm tired of being ticked off like an old clock.' That sent her off into peals of demented laughter.

'Quick, Vicky, she's going black in the face.' Dad rose out of his chair.

'Calm down. She's all right, aren't you, Gran?'

'They go round . . . telling . . . people . . . I d–r–i–n–k. Did you ever, hic, hear such . . . non . . . nonsense?' Gran looked pleadingly at Vicky, while her red face wobbled as if she were going to burst into tears. 'I don't do half what they . . . hic . . . say . . . I do. You know that . . . Vic . . . hic . . . ky.'

The familiar remark was poignant.

'C'mon, Gran. Let's get some air.' Vicky encircled her in her arms and took her off. When Gran's mind was focused on disaster there could be a hell of a row.

May and Tommy left at four o'clock for an unknown destination.

'Hollywood. That's where they're going,' said Jimmy Scanlon.

'Not till next month. It's the ring of Kerry now.' Mrs Tully could never keep anything to herself.

The old car swayed down the drive of the hotel, boots and cans rattling after it. The whole of Dun Laoghaire was there to wave them goodbye.

Vicky and I were alone in the bar having a quiet drink.

'Wonder what May's doing now?' I said.

'Driving to Kerry. But she'll never let him drive all that distance without stopping on the way,' Vicky giggled. 'Pete's looking wonderful.'

'Yes.'

'He seems to have recovered from the war.' Vicky was probing. 'There's no mistaking the way he looks at you. That's something the war didn't destroy. You should be grateful.'

'Vicky,' I hissed. 'Trust you to come out with something like that.'

'I speak as I find, as Gran would say, and seeing the way you blush, I know you know exactly what I mean.' We both laughed, relieving the tension. But I didn't tell her anything about Pete and me. I still didn't fully trust her.

The tables were cleared and at eight o'clock a three-piece band arrived. The dancing began. Pete didn't ask me to dance. He took possession of me and moved me on to the floor. His whole body came alive with the rhythm that had always inspired me.

'I'm sorry,' he buried his face in my hair. 'What I said was unforgivable. I came home specially to apologise.'

'I thought it was to see a real, live film star.'

He laughed.

We danced and in his arms I felt safe. He smiled a smile that conveyed to me that everything would be all right, and at that moment it was. He was close to me, solid and sinewy, and as I held him I realised how sad I'd be tomorrow when he'd gone.

Mam came to say they were leaving and gave Pete a withering look.

'She doesn't like me.'

'It's not that. She's just anxious that I finish my training.'

'I certainly won't stop you. I'm thinking of going to the States in a few months time anyway.'

'What?'

'Yes. Soon as I can get a visa. Detroit. That's where the

real money is. But I'll be waiting for you.'

The band played 'I can't stop loving you', and Pete held me close. There was no future for us. Mam had her sights set on a life for me that Pete Scanlon could only dream about, and at that moment I resented it.

'We can keep in touch, can't we?' Pete scribbled his address on a piece of paper and went to dance with Vicky.

'Will you take a slop to the floor?' May's Uncle Johnny up from the country was beside me. 'Or will ye sit there suckin' your mineral?'

'I'd love to dance Mr. . . .'

'Call me Johnny and don't mind if you get covered in hayseeds. They'll brush off.' He roared with laughter, his face purple, his two left feet sodden with the drink that dripped all the way down from his brain.

Later we said goodbye to Pete. I tried to sound as casual as I could.

'So long. Don't forget to write.' He addressed us both.

'We're always saying goodbye to Pete Scanlon,' Vicky mused.

'That's because he's always going away.'

'Well I won't follow him this time,' Vicky laughed. 'God, what a fool I made of myself that time.'

'Neither will I,' I said under my breath.

Mam was sitting in Gran's old chair by the Aga waiting up for us.

'What's wrong?' I checked the grandfather clock. It was almost one in the morning.

'There's a telegram from Karen. It came just as we got home.' She took the green envelope out of her pocket.

'Is it bad?'

Her eyes were dark and glittered in the firelight.

'No, I suppose not,' she sighed.

'You suppose?'

'Calm down, Lizzie. It's just to say that they're coming home.'

'Oh great. I can't wait to see them.'

'That's not all.'

The silence seemed interminable.

'What, Auntie Gertie? What?' Vicky prompted.

'She's bringing Hank, Paul's cousin with her. They're engaged. Didn't I tell you she wasn't staying on there just for the good of her health?' Her voice was resigned.

'That's wonderful news,' Vicky enthused.

'Yes. I suppose. She says she's never been happier.'

'When are they arriving?'

'Friday. Flying into Shannon. Then getting the train.'

'Great. I'll still be here,' said Vicky.

'You'll have a full house again, Mam. That should make you happy.'

'Yes it will. Meetings and partings from now on. Meetings and partings.'

She rose slowly from the chair and straightened herself.

'You'll probably be a bridesmaid again, Lizzie. What colour will you wear this time? We'll have to shop early. Get everything ready. Knowing Karen, she won't give us much time.'

'Don't think about it for the moment, Mam. You're tired. Here, have a cup of tea. Karen mightn't get married for ages yet.'

'She always plunged headlong into everything. And suffered the consequences.'

'It might work for her this time. She deserves a bit of happiness,' said Vicky.

'I wonder what Gran will make of all this?'

'She'll probably start making the cake. I'll help her. I know where the recipe is.' I went to the middle drawer of the dresser.

'I wish I could stay,' Vicky said. 'But I have to be back for college. I'll be home for your wedding, Lizzie. That's one event I wouldn't miss for the world.'

There was silence for a moment, then Mam said, 'You'll have plenty of time to save up. It won't be for years,' and shot me a knowing look. 'I wonder how John is? I can't wait to see the little lamb, neither can your dad.'

We talked and planned well into the early hours, each one of us too excited to go to bed. Karen's life had come full circle, and within that circle her joys and sorrows had nurtured my childhood. Lit by the love of our family, the circle widened to encompass those around us and their lives. I grew up in the light of their love. I was lucky.